"Dan, I Think I'd Better Go to My Room,"

she said, resisting when he urged her down on the beach lounger.

"Why, then? You've just admitted you can't breathe inside."

She was having even more trouble catching her breath out here, although she didn't dare tell him that.

"Emma, what are you afraid of?" he asked softly as his hands closed over her shoulders.

"I'm not afraid of anything," she lied valiantly.

"If you're not afraid of the dark, then it must be this you're afraid of." His mouth found hers, and with an impatient, muffled word, he drew her hard against his body. . . .

DIXIE BROWNING

is a native of North Carolina, and many of her stories are born as she travels from her home in Winston-Salem to her cottage in Frisco on Hatteras Island. "I have taken characters' names from mailboxes along my route," she confided. She is also an accomplished watercolor artist, as well as a writer.

D0830222

Dear Reader:

I'd like to take this opportunity to thank you for all your support and encouragement of Silhouette Romances.

Many of you write in regularly, telling us what you like best about Silhouette, which authors are your favorites. This is a tremendous help to us as we strive to publish the best contemporary romances possible.

All the romances from Silhouette Books are for you, so enjoy this book and the many stories to come. I hope you'll continue to share your thoughts with us, and invite you to write to us at the address below:

Karen Solem
Editor-in-Chief
Silhouette Books
P.O. Box 769
New York, N.Y. 10019

DIXIE BROWNING
Logic of the Heart

Silhouette *Romance*

Published by Silhouette Books New York

America's Publisher of Contemporary Romance

SILHOUETTE BOOKS, a Simon & Schuster Division of
GULF & WESTERN CORPORATION
1230 Avenue of the Americas, New York, N.Y. 10020

Copyright © 1982 by Dixie Browning

Distributed by Pocket Books

All rights reserved, including the right to reproduce
this book or portions thereof in any form whatsoever.
For information address Silhouette Books, 1230
Avenue of the Americas, New York, N.Y. 10020

ISBN: 0-671-57172-9

First Silhouette Books printing September, 1982

10 9 8 7 6 5 4 3 2 1

All of the characters in this book are fictitious. Any resemblance to actual persons, living or dead, is purely coincidental.

Map by Tony Ferrara

SILHOUETTE, SILHOUETTE ROMANCE and colophon are
registered trademarks of Simon & Schuster.

America's Publisher of Contemporary Romance

Printed in the U.S.A.

Other Silhouette Books by Dixie Browning

Unreasonable Summer
Tumbled Wall
Chance Tomorrow
Wren of Paradise
East of Today
Winter Blossom
Renegade Player
Island on the Hill

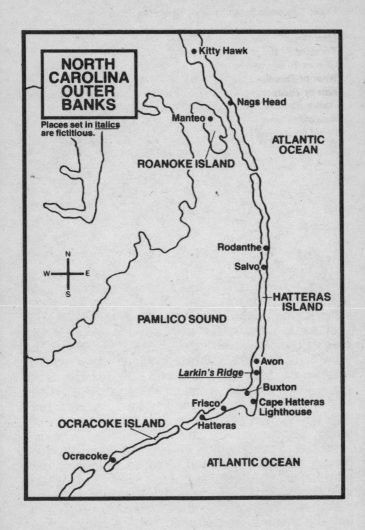

Chapter One

Emma automatically touched the brakes of her light blue Pinto to read the historical marker near Chicamacomico Coast Guard Station and just as automatically accelerated as the long line of cars behind her sounded their horns. It would have to wait until a time when traffic wasn't so thick on the road. Not for the first time, she wondered if she should have waited for the weekenders to be gone before making her way to the Outer Banks. In fact, for the past few hours she had been muttering aloud all the arguments pro and con for having taken the job in the first place. It had been one more of her leap-before-you-look impulses that had taken root the first time Rosie had mentioned it.

For one thing, it hadn't come through the usual channels at TempSec, where Emma was listed for hire as a short-term secretary, so the agency wasn't too happy about her going. For another, even her apartment mate, Rosie Fischer, who had been offered the job in the first place, had warned her about working for Margo Summerlin.

But then there was her stepbrother Hugh, who had been pathetically grateful when she had promised to help bail him out of his latest escapade.

It had started when Hugh had gotten himself into debt at a private gambling club—thanks to his unfortunate penchant for gaming with more enthusiasm than skill—and the manager, Derek Villers, had taken an uncomfortable interest in Emma.

At first she had been mildly flattered, for Derek Villers would be considered by some women to be attractive, despite his thickening waistline and an irritatingly overfamiliar manner. But now she could hardly wait until she could pay back every cent Hugh owed the man and be done with his increasingly pressing attentions. To Emma's distress, her stepbrother was spending more and more time with the older man. Emma was not sure whether this was Hugh's idea or Derek's; all she knew was that she didn't dare risk an open confrontation with the club manager. If he decided to press the matter of Hugh's debt, her brother's career as an accountant would be over before it even got off the ground. He had been hired shortly after graduation by an accounting firm, with a good chance of advancement. Unfortunately, few employers looked with benevolence on an accountant who couldn't pass up a game of chance if his life depended on it.

The National Park Service Campground at Salvo was filling up rapidly and Emma realized that if Margo Summerlin proved as unpleasant a person as Rosie had declared, she might find herself seeking shelter here instead of enjoying the spacious live-in accommodations that were promised as part of the job benefits. That had been a large part of the lure—six weeks at the beach working for television's Margo Summerlin, drawing top wages and having all her expenses taken care of. In spite of what Rosie had said, Emma had thoroughly enjoyed the interview programs she had seen with the lovely blond television star cleverly bringing out aspects of her various subjects that had not been revealed before. Thinking back to the last program she had seen, Emma was a little surprised to find that she had forgotten the subject of the interview and all that she could recall was the image of Margo, looking chic and glamorous in a white safari suit against a background of bombed-out buildings.

After working for a day, a week, or a month for a series of visiting politicians and traveling businessmen through TempSec, Emma would enjoy this brush with glamour. For a girl who had grown up, gone to school, and worked in New York City and Washington, D.C., she had discovered little of the legendary romance those cities were reputed to have. Now, after years of feeling dwarfed by skyscrapers, of straphanging and wrestling for parking spaces, of tottering along in her high heels on hard, hot pavements, she was going to take off her shoes and let down her hair, both literally and figuratively. Her hard-earned skills as a secretary had afforded her this chance and she wasn't going to pass it up.

Rosie, who worked as a pool secretary at the studio where Margo was under contract, had been called to the office and told that Margo Summerlin, vacationing on the Outer Banks of North Carolina, needed a secretary and had asked for Fischer. Rosie had proclaimed herself not available, giving some family-related excuse, although telling Emma privately that if wild dogs were after her she wouldn't voluntarily shut herself up for six weeks with Summerlin, no matter how much she was offered, but Emma was not so timid. Not for nothing did she have hair that glowed with smoldering fire under the prosaic brown, and anyone who could have seen her at that moment would have immediately recognized the light of determination in her slanted green eyes. Her rounded chin, whose strength was only slightly mitigated by a shallow dimple, indicated more belligerence than was usually found in so tiny a package. She might be small, but she wasn't one to back down from a challenge and she had challenged herself to take everything Margo Summerlin could dish out *and* do a flawless job as a secretary *and* have herself one whale of a good summer in a completely new environment.

She checked off the landmarks; past the now privately owned Kinnakeet Coast Guard Sta-

tion—that had to be it, with the lookout tower off
to one side; past the village of Avon—did that
theater really say Stratford-at-Avon? It did, and
there, in sight of the towering black-and-white-
striped lighthouse, was the small sign that announced Larkin's Ridge. *Cottage* was not a word
she would have chosen to describe the house. It
wasn't at all what she expected—not perched up
on a dune, as she had hoped, but on the Sound
side of the narrow island. Still, it was in sight of
the Atlantic, for there was nothing between it
and the ocean except the orderly progression of
sea-oat-covered dunes, and behind it a creek cut
in from the Pamlico, gleaming like pewter in the
low, dense vegetation. There were several small
boats moored along the sides of the creek, including, to her delight, a small sailboat. Emma
tried to maintain a cool, unexcited mien as she
climbed stiffly from behind the wheel.

The door was painted an unusual shade of
gray-green that matched the window trim, the
storm shutters, and the cupola that surmounted
the middle section of the weathered shingled
house. Emma glanced appreciatively about her
at the inviting-looking screened porch as she
clanged on the bronze bell once more.

When no one answered her noisy summons,
she shrugged and returned dejectedly to her car.
Before she could climb inside, she heard the
sound of childish laughter coming from somewhere out in back of the house. Halfway around,
she decided reluctantly that she was going to
have to relinquish her ego-supporting heels for
the time being. They were not the thing for

trudging through deep sand and so she slipped them off and left them beside the narrow footpath as she followed the sound of voices.

"Look at this one, Uncle Dan—he's going to have babies," piped a clear boyish tone.

"*She's* getting ready to *spawn*, Dennis. Minor difference, perhaps, but important," indulgently corrected an amused baritone. "That's the roe. The babies, when they hatch out, will be called fry."

"Then why don't you say she's rowing?" asked the child with what Emma felt was perfect logic. "And if we fry her babies . . ."

Emma listened with growing amusement as the child backed his uncle into a semantic corner as she found her way through the thick grove of fragrant bushes to a clearing. She looked down on two backs, equally bare and equally bronzed, but there the similarity ended. Both males were seated on low wooden boxes in shallow water and they were doing something with heaps of silver-sided fish, the child wielding a knife with a dexterity that amazed her.

They both looked up at the same time and Emma found herself coloring as two sets of chocolate dark eyes surveyed her with masculine frankness. The only difference was that the child's gaze was openly friendly and the man's registered a faintly hostile questioning.

She stopped where she was, on the bank above where they sat, and refusing to be put off by the man's attitude, she announced herself. "Hello. I'm Emma Tamplin and I'm looking for Margo Summerlin. Is this the right place?" she asked, her determined smile hardly wavering as the man stood to face her. Both man and boy were clad alike in filthy jeans, their thick black hair wind tumbled and just slightly longer than the well-kept city-style cuts she was accustomed to.

"Miss Summerlin isn't here at the moment. I'm Dan Slater." He indicated the boy beside him. "My nephew, Dennis. May I help you?"

Feeling slightly intimidated as a hoard of screeching gulls swooped down from out of nowhere, Emma looked anxiously from one to the other. "Oh, but . . . well, do you know when she'll be coming back? I'm her new secretary. At least, I'm hoping to be," she added as doubts began to pile up inside her. The Slater man looked as if he had never heard of a secretary and didn't much care for the species now that he had met one face to face.

"Margo's gone back to Washington," the boy volunteered as the two adults surveyed one another cautiously.

Dan Slater, Emma observed, was a man of perhaps thirty-five or so, darkly attractive without being precisely handsome. His eyes were piercing under his thick, arched brows and his chin was altogether too aggressive for comfort. He was slightly taller than average, as far as she could judge from her higher vantage point, compactly muscled, and his lean hips and widely braced legs in close-fitting jeans hinted at a masculine virility she found hard to ignore.

Suddenly, Emma wondered uncomfortably how she had fared after a trip of several hours' duration. When she had left Washington early that morning her mirror had revealed a nicely curved five feet and three quarters of an inch of

attractive femininity, neatly dressed in a leaf-
print cotton voile that made the most of her
ivory complexion without unduly emphasizing
the scattering of seasonal freckles that adorned
her short, straight nose. Now, however, with her
feet unfortunately bare and her hair wildly
windblown, she must look like the least efficient
of secretaries and it was pure nervousness that
made her rush into speech under the pressure of
the level dark scrutiny.

"The secretary Miss Summerlin asked for
couldn't come, you see, but I was free and my
speeds are every bit as good as . . . and I've done
some work once or twice before for people in the
television industry and so the . . . the terms
won't be all that unfamiliar to me. I . . . Miss
Summerlin does still need me, doesn't she?"
That last sounded disgustingly plaintive to her
own ears and she tried to excuse herself on the
grounds that she was hot, tired, and extremely
hungry, and it didn't help matters to be greeted
by two half-naked throwbacks to an age of pira-
cy. It wasn't as if she were one of those gung-ho
summer camp types who could splice a mast
and batten a bilge with the best of them . . . or
whatever it was they did, she thought defensively. It wasn't her fault her parents had been city
birds and she had never spent more than the
occasional weekend in the country; the Slater
man didn't have to examine her as if she had
just stepped off a flying saucer.

"Miss Summerlin will be back either tomorrow or the next day. She had some tapes to
remake at the studio, but you're welcome to wait
for her, Miss . . . Tamplin?"

Emma nodded and he continued. "It's just that I wasn't expecting a secretary, since Miss Summerlin is on vacation, and Dennis and I aren't exactly in a condition to welcome a guest at the moment."

"But then, I'm not exactly a guest," Emma replied, beginning to enjoy the sensation of looking down on someone for a change. "This *is* Miss Summerlin's house, though, isn't it? I was given rather explicit instructions and I'm usually pretty good at following directions."

"You followed them perfectly this time, Miss Tamplin," Dan Slater said, leaping lightly up the embankment and spoiling Emma's exalted viewpoint. "Only this isn't Miss Summerlin's house—it's mine. Miss Summerlin is my guest and as her secretary you're welcome, of course. If you'll come along, I'll show you to a room." He turned to the boy behind him. "Dennis, scale them and I'll be back to dress them."

Slanting a sidelong look at the powerfully defined profile, Emma thought about warning him that a child that age—Dennis looked to be about eight—shouldn't be left unsupervised with a knife almost as long as his arm, but she kept quiet. Both Dan and Dennis Slater were completely outside her own experience and she was beginning to think the men she was apt to run into here on the Outer Banks might be a breed apart from any she had dealt with in the past.

They went in through the back door, with Emma feeling slightly at a disadvantage carrying her shoes in her hand. While she wasn't unduly sensitive about her lack of inches, she nevertheless felt better able to cope with situations when she stood as high as her heels could lift her. Besides which, she must look silly in her frilly voile dress with her feet bare and paler than the sand they walked through.

She told him when he asked that her car was in front of the house and that her bags were in it and he left her at the door of a surprisingly lovely bedroom—although why she should be surprised wasn't quite clear to her. While the man himself appeared to be a rough diamond at best, the house was charming, and by no stretch of imagination could it be considered a fisherman's shack.

The kitchen they had passed through had whitewashed paneling with colorful rag rugs on the floor and generous touches of copper. It had contained every imaginable appliance, but it was badly in need of a thorough cleaning. By contrast, the room she surveyed now was in mint condition, it's paneling polished to an almost translucent glow and the antique pine furniture and brass bed set off by pristine white spread, draperies, and rugs. It was also unused, if the slight mustiness was anything to go by, and she crossed to open both windows and allow the fragrant breeze to lift the curtains.

Whoever Mrs. Slater was, Emma admired her taste in furnishings, although she deplored her housekeeping standards if the kitchen was anything to go by.

"This all?" the man asked, putting her two bags down on the chest at the foot of the bed. "Bath's through there if you don't mind sharing with Dennis. Miss Summerlin has the suite on the other side of Dennis's room and I'll show you where you'll be working when you've had time to freshen up. Now, if you'll excuse me, I'll go finish up the fish before Dennis decides to do the job alone."

His absence left an echo in the quiet atmosphere of the room, a disturbingly masculine presence that made her glad to see the back of him. It was almost as if she could see the imprint of his brown, high-arched foot against the white crocheted rug beside the bed, and there was a faint aroma of fish, sweat, and pine-scented soap that, oddly enough, she found not at all unpleasant.

Shaking herself out of the strange mood with a small, breathless laugh, Emma unpacked her bags and washed up, changing into a dark green slacks suit with a halter top. Not very business-like, she thought, but if her host could greet her in nothing but filthy jeans, she might just as well get into the swing of things by trying out her newly purchased beachwear. She had bought little enough, for the main purpose of this six-week assignment was to earn enough money to get Hugh out from under the influence of Derek Villers. Then, if they had to, they might both relocate and start all over again somewhere where every time the doorbell sounded Emma didn't feel herself tighten up in fear of the insidiously friendly man.

She heard the two Slaters let themselves in the back door as she put the finishing touches to her face—a light dusting of powder to subdue her few freckles and a dash of lip gloss on lips that were naturally red. Her brows and lashes

were dark enough to need no help and the same
summer warmth that added to her crop of freckles had a way of bringing color to her thin
complexion too readily for her to need to resort to
the use of a blusher.

Feeling slightly like a trespasser, she made
her way back to the kitchen. After all, she had
not yet been shown over the rest of the house
and it seemed presumptuous on her part to
simply make herself at home, especially as she
had met neither her hostess nor her employer so
far. What the relationship between Margo Summerlin and the Slaters was, she couldn't imagine, for the sophisticated television star with her
streaked blond hair and her long, perfectly oval
face certainly bore no resemblance to the
brawny dark Dan Slater, nor to his smaller
edition, Dennis. Of course, she could just as well
be related to Mrs. Slater . . . or they could be
simply friends.

Pretty good friends, though, to offer to put up
with both a guest and the guest's secretary for
six weeks.

"Hi, Miss Tamplin," the boy greeted her.
"Uncle Dan and I are going to fry bluefish for
supper. Can you make cornbread or hushpuppies?"

"Can I . . . ? Oh. Cooking, you mean," Emma
said, grinning. "Well. I've never attempted cornbread but if you'll point me in the direction of a
cookbook and a stove, I'll do my best."

"Recipes," the boy sneered. "Martha never
uses recipes."

Dan turned away from the sink, where he had
been sloshing water liberally over face, arms,

and chest. He stood there unabashedly drying himself in front of her as if they weren't perfect strangers and Emma wondered just what she had let herself in for by coming here to live in a house with people she knew nothing about.

"I'd better fill you in on the situation here, Miss Tamplin," Dan offered, his opaque eyes registering neither eagerness nor reluctance to do so. "Martha Gallins is my housekeeper. Unfortunately, the day after Miss Summerlin arrived Martha had to . . . leave. I don't know quite when she'll be back, but until she returns Dennis and I are batching it. If you'd care to pitch in and help, you're welcome. If not, you'll just have to take potluck—or eat out."

His attitude said, Take it or leave it, and Emma, slightly stung by his unconcern, decided she'd take it. What's more, she'd pitch in and help. She might not be the world's most experienced cook, but she could read and follow instructions and she could darned well do a better job of cleaning up than either of the Slaters could.

The cornbread wasn't half bad and the fish was delicious, the best she had ever eaten. Dennis regaled her while they devoured it with the details of how they had caught them in the gillnet his uncle had set out near the channel. When he went on to describe the gar that had seemed intent on attacking the net while they were fishing it and the hard crabs that ate the catch if they didn't check it every two or three hours, Emma turned with determined cheerfulness to the older Slater with a question about the weather. She preferred to do without the intimate details of how the filet came to be on her plate.

That night she slept soundly as soon as her head touched the pillow, due more to her own tiredness than to the Dubonnet and tonic water she sipped while Dan poured himself a stiffer nightcap. The boy had gone to bed readily at a nod from his uncle and Emma wondered if he had bothered to wash up and brush his teeth, but she felt it wasn't her place to question the casual relationship between the two of them.

Dan had excused himself early on the pretext of having work to do and Emma, feeling deserted, had listened to his laborious two-finger typing coming from behind a closed door and been tempted to offer her help, but her own weariness hit her suddenly and she went to bed, feeling vaguely incomplete.

It was only that she hadn't said an official good night to her host, she told herself as she made ready for bed, and that she had yet to meet her hostess, who, for all she knew, might have gone to Washington with Margo Summerlin. She had cleared away the dishes, plus the several days of neglect, and both Slaters had offered perfunctory thanks, but that was all. No excuses, no explanations. Perhaps the Banks bred a particularly chauvinistic strain of men, who took woman's place in the kitchen for granted, she thought with sleepy amusement just before her eyelids settled for the night. An incredibly soft breeze lifted the muslin curtains and she slept to the muffled roar of the ocean.

It took several minutes for Emma to become oriented when first she opened her eyes the next morning, and when she finally recalled all that had taken place yesterday, she sat up, deter-mined to cook a good breakfast for the Slater males. She might not be a dab hand at corn-bread, but she could make a delicious omelet and fry bacon to perfection.

She bathed hastily, and dressed in the same slacks suit she had worn the night before. It was styled so that it could be dressed up or down; she hadn't known last night whether or not Dan and Dennis would come to the table in their jeans with no shirts. Even though they had dined in the kitchen instead of the lovely dining room she had discovered, both men had changed into something more respectable.

In Dan's case it had also been more disturb-ing. The crisp white shirt set off his dark, angu-lar features and emphasized the slightly distant attitude that he wore like a second skin, in spite of his surface pleasantries.

On the table she had left sparkling clean the night before were now two mugs, two bowls, and a scattering of dry cereal, attesting to the fact that the Slaters had already breakfasted. Telling herself that she was glad to be spared the trou-ble, Emma fixed herself a cup of coffee and wandered outdoors nibbling on a peach and a slice of cheddar. The hint of disappointment was only because she was in the habit of sharing breakfast with Rosie in their cramped apart-ment. She certainly didn't expect the Slaters to drop everything and entertain her when she wasn't even their guest.

She wasn't anyone's guest, come to that—merely an employee whose employer hadn't shown up yet in a house without a hostess. An invidious position, but she had weathered far more awkward situations in her twenty-four years and she was determined to enjoy this period at the beach, come what may. It might be a long time before she found herself here again and she wasn't one to waste her opportunities.

Nor was she one to impose without trying to make restitution. So after clearing away the breakfast things, she made her own bed and straightened the bathroom, finding evidence that Dennis had indeed washed the night before when she saw the filthy towel behind the door. She smiled as she spread it out to dry before dropping it in the hamper and on impulse wandered through the door on the other side of the bathroom. She wished she hadn't.

The boy's room was a disaster area and it was beyond her to ignore it. Some twenty minutes later she closed the door behind her and stood in the hallway, wondering what to do next. She had been hired as a secretary, not as a maid-of-all-work, but she might as well make herself useful, if only to pay her room and board until her actual duties began. By that time, the redoubtable Martha would be in residence again and she would have only her own room to see to.

The door opposite her room was ajar, pushed, no doubt, by the breeze that drifted steadily through the well-ventilated house, and Emma found herself standing in the doorway without consciously having moved. It was not as bad, certainly, as Dennis's room, but the dark brown sheets on the bed had been left tumbled and the jeans that Dan Slater had shucked off still lay on the floor, along with a pair of paint-stained khakis. There was a half-smoked cigar in an ashtray and the breeze was drifting the ashes across the dusty table.

Emma's hand automatically strayed to the bed and she smoothed the sheet, then bent and swept it up vigorously, tucking the foot in and plumping the pillows, and the rest followed as a matter of course. By the time she was finished, the brown and white room with its touches of turquoise looked as tidy as did Dennis's and her own when she stood back to survey it. It occurred to her that this was the room of a man of sophisticated tastes, the books, artifacts, and accessories revealing that not all Dan Slater's traveling was done between the back yard and his gillnet.

There were no indications of feminine habitation—no toiletries, nor any dressing table where they could be kept out of sight. The one closet, when she slowly opened the door, revealed only masculine attire—several pairs of slacks, a waterproof jacket, and, oddly enough, a three-piece suit of a finely textured material whose expert tailoring announced itself even on the hanger. Shoes were neatly aligned on the floor—a pair of moccasins, two pairs of deck shoes, and a pair of tan brogans that were plainly bench made. Behind them was a briefcase of the same tan leather.

Hearing a door slam, Emma stepped back, suddenly aware of just what she was doing. Wild color flooded her face and she turned to leave the room when the door was pushed further open and she found herself face to face with an extremely forbidding-looking Dan Slater.

"Were you looking for me?" he asked, his narrowed eyes sweeping the newly tidied room.

"No, I . . . that is . . ." she stumbled, hating the fact that her thin skin served as a barometer for her every emotional change.

One black eyebrow lifted derisively and she felt like slinking away, tail between her legs. As that wasn't possible, she straightened her shoulders, uncomfortably aware of their pale bareness, and jutted her chin to make herself taller. "I decided to repay your hospitality," she told him firmly. "Well, actually, I picked up Dennis's towel in the bathroom and then I saw his room and . . . well, one thing led to another and here I am—all finished up. And now, if you'll excuse me, I'd like to . . ." What would she like to do? She couldn't think of a single thing—at least, nothing that wasn't wildly unreasonable.

"Thank you, Miss Tamplin," Dan Slater said gravely. "I'll show you where you'll be working. Then, as Miss Summerlin's not here yet, you might like to look around the island. One of the nicer things about Hatteras Island is the fact that there are still miles of empty beach where you can walk or swim without stumbling over all the sun-worshiping bodies."

"I . . . thank you, Mr. Slater. I'd like that. If you'll just point me in the right direction, I'll wander around and see what's to be seen."

"Dennis and I will give you the guided tour," he told her quietly, his tone leaving no room for argument.

* * *

The guided tour began with a drive through the village of Avon, or, as Dan explained the common use of its original name, Kinnakeet. From there they drove on down the beach toward the lighthouse and, with Dennis bouncing excitedly on the back seat of the jeep, Dan told her about the tallest lighthouse in North America. He described the times when it had been in and out of use, due to the Second World War and its blackouts, and mentioned the constant threat of erosion as the greedy Atlantic ate away at the sands that supported its monumental stone base.

They stopped in the visitor's center and walked the nature trail, an enchanting microcosm of the maritime forest that covered miles of the lower part of the island. After that, they drove south to Hatteras village, where they had lunch and then took the free ferry to Ocracoke.

On board the ferry, Emma got out with Dennis and stood at the stern, tossing leftover hushpuppies he had saved from lunch to the hungry flock of following gulls. They giggled together when one particularly bold beggar swooped to steal a morsel from another gull and lost it to a third. Then, feeling an exhilaration brought on by sun and spray and the clean beauty of the island, Emma held both her hands over her head with the last of her crumbs.

Something hit her in the back and she gasped, feeling a hard arm go around her to drag her away from the heavy chain across the stern. "You idiot—did it ever occur to you that you might need your fingers again?" Dan Slater demanded furiously. He was holding her against him as if afraid she might bolt, and she sagged there, her heart pounding in her chest as she struggled to catch her breath.

"You didn't have to scare me to death," she accused, twisting her head to glare up at him.

"If you don't have enough common sense to take care of yourself, someone else has to do it," he informed her coldly.

She looked frantically around for Dennis only to find that, like the rest of the passengers, he had moved to the side of the ferry to wave to the people on the returning ferry. At the moment she and Dan were quite alone. "I didn't see a sign that said please don't feed the birds," she muttered, trying to wrest herself away from his iron grip.

There was no reply, and when she slanted him a rebellious look she caught an expression on his face that puzzled her long after the day's sightseeing was done. "Toss it. Don't hold it," was all he said, though.

They went on to Ocracoke, seeing several Banker ponies along the way, remnants of a herd of wild mustangs that had roamed the islands for generations. Dan Slater was a perfect guide—informative, untiring, and completely impersonal. He carefully avoided touching her again, but on several occasions she was aware of his dark enigmatic eyes following her when she moved off to examine a rack of postcards or to study the marine growth on a submerged piling.

By the time they reached Larkin's Ridge once more, her mind was overflowing with information about the fascinating history of the Banks. As she lay in her bed that night, however, it wasn't the bits and pieces of history she heard in her mind, but the musical cadence of Dan's voice with its tantalizing touch of a brogue that was much more pronounced in young Dennis.

Chapter Two

By the time the sun struck the curtains of her east window, Emma was awake, her mind picking up the threads of the day before as if she had only closed her eyes for a moment, instead of sinking immediately into a deep and dreamless sleep. She had learned almost by accident—for Dan was not a man to talk about himself—that he was originally from the island and had lived in Washington for the past several years, but that was all. She didn't even know whether or not he was married, although she rather thought not. There was something untamed about the man that could almost be taken as a challenge by any woman worth her salt. Emma had to remind herself that her present concern was to try and earn enough in six weeks to get herself and her stepbrother out from under the insidious influence of Derek Villers.

Turning over restlessly, she burrowed her chin on her fists and allowed herself to relive the first time she had ever met the man. Hugh had phoned her just as she stepped out of the shower to say that he needed her and could she come immediately. She had thought at first he meant for her to come to the room he rented several blocks away from her own apartment, but he explained to her that he was in a hotel and gave her the address and the room number and asked her to bring all the money she had on her . . . please.

She had piled her wet hair under a scarf and dressed hurriedly in slacks and a polo coat, torn between anxiety and irritation. It had seemed a good idea for Hugh to join her in Washington after he finished school, for they were practically alone in the world since her father and his mother had moved to the West Coast a year earlier. But as she grew to know her stepbrother better as an adult, she couldn't help but worry about some element of . . . was it irresponsibility? . . . in his makeup.

Whatever it was, he was her brother, if only by marriage, and she had backed her light blue Pinto into the street shortly after nine that night. The automobile was her one extravagance, but she had soon discovered that working, as she did, first one place, then another, it made more sense to have her own transportation than to try and figure bus routes out each time.

The hotel was one of a lesser chain and Emma had wondered what on earth could have brought Hugh here at this time of night. She made her way to the proper room and rapped on the door and was instantly greeted by an anxious-looking Hugh. He pulled her into the room and introduced her to a man of some forty years, a tall, slightly fleshy man who greeted her pleasantly enough while he examined her with the ease of long practice.

It seemed that Derek Villers was the manager of a private club where there was high-stakes gambling and Hugh had had the misfortune to get in over his head several weeks earlier and was having no luck at all in paying off his debts.

Much later, Emma had come to wonder if Derek Villers didn't encourage just such irresponsibility, for he seemed to take a perverse sort of pleasure in his power over the two young people. It seemed to satisfy some obscure need in the man to alternately offer encouragement— "It's nobody's business but my own if I want to be generous to my friends"—and veiled threats—"It's not up to me—I'm only the manager."

Once he had met Emma, she had known no peace, for he called her often, reporting on her brother's efforts to work off his debt by doing bookkeeping at the club. He usually wanted to take her out to dinner and she refused him as often as she dared, but there was something about the man—some trick he had of bringing up Hugh's awkward position—that frightened her. She felt as if she had to stay on the right side of him until her brother was out from under his thumb.

That first night—that had been when she discovered to her acute embarrassment that she was very photogenic. They had been leaving the hotel together, with Derek Villers insisting on walking them out to her car, when they stepped out into the parking lot and were immediately caught up in the aftermath of a demonstration of some sort. Flash bulbs were popping as police sorted out the mob, and Emma had been chagrined to see her own face staring wide-eyed at her over coffee the next morning. Derek and Hugh had been holding her back protectively as they saw what was going on and the expression on each of their three faces was clearly evident behind the police activity in the foreground— Derek looked extremely annoyed, Hugh looked thoroughly ashamed, and Emma, through some fluke of lighting, looked beautiful and arrogant. It had been that instinctive defensiveness of hers, of course—a way she had of greeting trouble with her head thrown back, as if to make up for her size. Hugh had once likened her to a bantam hen with her feathers all ruffled and she supposed she was.

"Emma?" came a boyish voice through her bedroom door, breaking her away from her uncomfortable reverie.

"Hi, Dennis. Ready for breakfast?" she called back, swinging her feet to the floor.

"Gosh, no! We had that an hour ago. We're getting ready to go tend the net and Uncle Dan said I could ask you if you wanted to come. You do, don't you?"

Weighing reluctance against a natural curiosity and a strong desire to see Dan again, she said she'd love to. "Give me five minutes," she sang out, already heading for the bathroom.

"You're an idiot, Emma Tamplin," she accused herself, for she knew that Margo Summerlin would be back sometime today, but she was determined to spend as much time with Dan Slater as she could, and if that meant plucking fish from a net from the shaky security of a small boat, then that's what she'd do.

It was a new experience, she rationalized, and Emma had never backed down from a new experience—except in the line of romance. She and Rosie had seen eye to eye on that score, both feeling that they wanted to wait for something lasting instead of falling in and out of affairs like so many of their contemporaries.

The trip in Dan's skiff out to the net took less than ten minutes and then Emma watched while the boy grabbed at a scarlet float with a flag on top, and when Dan cut the engine, they began to pull the boat along by the corked line that floated on the surface. The first time she saw one of the glittering fish caught by the gills she drew back instinctively, but soon she began to watch eagerly for the first glimpse of them. Then, before she quite knew it, she was mimicking the actions of the two Slaters and grabbing at the fish that came within her reach, squeezing and twisting to untangle them from the net. Dan insisted she wear his gloves and she caught a gleam of amusement in eyes that just might have been touched with admiration. She wondered if he had expected her to shudder and quail, knowing her for the city girl she was, and she was determined not to give him cause to despise her.

By the time they reached the anchor end, with both boxes filled with fish, Emma was as filthy as the Slaters were, for the stiff southwest wind blew silt, sea grass, and things she preferred not to dwell on, and they were all bespattered and in high spirits when they idled into the creek once more.

Dan hopped overboard in the shallow water and pulled the skiff up closer to the bank, leaving Dennis to do mysterious things to the engine. Without quite knowing how it came about, Emma found herself seated between the two Slaters, with young Dennis showing her how to scale the blues, trout, and croakers. They worked on a sort of assembly line, and soon the two boxes of fish had been reduced to a single heap of filets.

While Dan, followed by a hoard of greedy gulls, ran the scraps back out to where another fisherman worked his crab pots, Dennis and Emma washed the fish and wrapped them for freezing. Then Dan was back and all three of them helped wash down the skiff before making their way up to the house.

Somewhere along the way Dan had lost his usual cloak of reserve and he was laughing as freely at Emma's bedraggled appearance as was Dennis. They reached the back door and Dennis turned on the hose as a matter of course, and so they took turns, with Emma squealing as the cold jet of water was turned on her. She danced around, sputtering laughter, totally oblivious to the fact that her wet clothes clung to her with a faithfulness that revealed every line of her small body. When it was her turn to play the stream of water over Dan, she couldn't help but notice the magnificent way his wet chest and shoulders gleamed like polished copper under the morning sun.

Dennis had dashed inside, claiming he was going to get his camera and take a picture of them, and still laughing, Emma tried to part Dan's hair with the jet of water. He ducked away, got a faceful, and then grabbed her arm to wrest the hose away from her. It was only natural for her to resist. She held the hose behind her and when Dan's arms went around her to grab her wrist, she found herself brought up against his solid body and she caught her breath, shivering with something more than just the icy water.

It saved laundry, she supposed, for the Slaters to tend their net in jeans, leaving their shirts ashore, but when Emma found her face only inches from the fine pelt of body hair that swirled on Dan's chest to taper off beneath his jeans, she found her breath doing funny things in her throat. When she saw the rapid flutter of a pulse beneath his tanned skin, she tried to back away only to come up against the restraint of his arms.

"I . . . I'd better go inside and . . . and feed Dennis," she murmured distractedly, pressing herself away from him.

"He's taken to you." Dan's eyes played over her dripping face, touched on her sodden mop of hair, and returned to linger on her mouth.

"I've taken to him, too," she managed in a tone totally unlike her usual firm one.

"He's going to be with me a month while his parents are in Europe," Dan told her, his words seeming strangely disassociated from the eyes that roamed over her quite openly.

"That's nice."

Their bodies were so close she could feel the heat emanating from him. Dan held her wrist and she was leaning back against his arm, prey to a shattering array of sensations as they stood there, frozen motionless in the brisk, bright morning light.

"Uncle Dan," interjected a childish voice, "did you know the hose has squirted through the window and the curtains are all wet and I can't find my camera since my room got all cleaned?"

The childish protest broke through the barrier of her dazed consciousness and Emma escaped to the kitchen, where she concentrated on preparing Dennis's dinner.

The rest of the day she managed to avoid Dan. Utterly confused by the emotions he could arouse in her without even trying, she maintained her distance while she did her best to sort them out. After clearing away the lunch things, she walked across the highway to the beach and Dennis, who asked to come with her, was told by his uncle that he was needed to help work on a pump.

To her chagrin, Dan seemed equally intent on avoiding *her* and she sat on top of a dune until the greenheads discovered her and drove her down to the surf; then she walked for miles with the water seething whitely over her feet and, as the wind picked up, got herself liberally sprayed with salt.

By the time she returned to the house, she was tired out. The invigorating salt air and the unaccustomed exercise had done its job, and even though it was time to help fix dinner, Emma could not bring herself to do more than sprawl across her bed. She slept heavily, her damp clothes clinging to her as the breeze dried them stiffly on her body. Somewhere along the line she woke enough to hear voices coming from the kitchen, but nothing could stir her from her torpor.

The late afternoon sun that had slanted across her bed earlier, warming her as she lay there in her damp clothing, had moved on to leave a slight chill, but it wasn't the chill that woke her.

"Miss Tamplin?" came a voice that was familiar and unfamiliar at the same time. "I think there's been some sort of mistake. If I'd wanted an agency secretary, I'd have gotten in touch with an agency. I asked for Fischer and instead I got some little typist who won't be the slightest use to me."

Emma, who had been sleeping on her back with her hair spread out around her head to dry, opened her eyes to see Margo Summerlin standing over her, long, golden tanned hands firmly on her hips. She blinked awake, struggling to reconcile the image of one of television's loveliest stars with this sharp-tongued woman who leaned over her, eyes blazing contemptuously and glossy lips thinned to an ominous line.

From that moment on, as if a treacherous current had suddenly cut through the warm, lazy waters at Larkin's Ridge, the atmosphere changed. Dennis glanced up with an almost guilty look when Emma came into the living room after showering and changing, and after a mumbled excuse, he hurried from the room.

Dan was nowhere in sight. To Emma's acute

discomfort, only Margo Summerlin was present. The older woman was standing in front of the windows, her white-clad legs assuming a stance that automatically put her in control of the situation. From where Emma stood hesitantly in the doorway she could see a stream of smoke blown to one side of that elegant blond head. Then the woman turned to confront her, her face hardly more friendly than when she had awakened Emma fifteen minutes before.

"Well? What do you have to say for yourself?" she demanded, putting Emma on the defensive for whatever unknown crime she seemed to have committed.

"I'm afraid I don't know what you mean," Emma came back, determined not to be intimidated. She might be small, but few people had been able to push her around against her will.

"I sent for Fischer because I wanted Fischer, not some itinerant typist with a mistaken notion of knocking out a few smudgy, misspelled letters for me in between trips to the beach."

Thankful for the support of the three-inch heels she habitually wore to overcome her lack of inches, Emma stretched herself to her most impressive height and answered with far more calm than she felt. "Rosie wasn't able to come and she understood you needed someone as quickly as possible," she said, failing to mention the reason her friend had declined the doubtful honor. "As I'm a perfectly capable secretary with two years training and three years experience, I took her place. If you don't need me after all, I'll go back and let you . . ."

She had actually turned to go when Margo's

words caught up with her. "You'll do no such thing! We'll see just how competent you are, Miss . . . whatever your name is . . . and in the meantime, there won't be an opportunity for you to make a nuisance of yourself with Mr. Slater, because I'll see that you stay busy enough not to forget who you are and why you're here! You can get to work tonight after dinner and then I'll see you every morning at nine."

The golden brown eyes that had looked so attractive on television suddenly narrowed and she jabbed her cigarette out impatiently in the salt-glazed bowl on the coffee table. "Don't I know you from somewhere?" she demanded. "Do you work for my television station?"

When Emma shook her head and answered that she worked for TempSec, Margo Summerlin frowned slightly and muttered that she never forgot a face and that she'd remember sooner or later.

"I have done some work for another station. Maybe . . ."

"It's not important. All right, Tamplin, you can go now, but come to my office after dinner and I'll spell out your duties." With a regal nod of her golden blond head, the older woman dismissed her.

On the other side of the door, Emma expelled her breath in a gust, sorely tempted to walk out and not look back. Of all the . . . She couldn't say Rosie hadn't warned her, but all the same, nothing in the series of popular programs Emma had seen had prepared her for the reality of Margo Summerlin. She had heard of people who climbed to the top of the heap over the battered bodies of their minions, but this was the first time she had actually seen an example. Not that climbing over the negligible body of one Emma Tamplin would raise Margo much higher in the world, Emma thought wryly with a return to her natural good humor.

She was determined not to back down, and not just because of the money, either, which was half again as much as she usually earned, but because she wouldn't be able to hold her head up if she allowed herself to be defeated by someone like Margo Summerlin. The minute she started responding with her emotions instead of her reason she'd be in trouble.

Look at her own father. Ed Tamplin had the same impulsive, headlong streak she had inherited and it had manifested itself in gambling— the same weakness that had ironically shown up in his stepson.

No, there was a dark side to the Tamplin nature and the only way she could combat it, according to her levelheaded stepmother, was to keep her feet firmly on the ground and her head in control at all times. That did *not* allow any room for throwing up a perfectly good job because of a sharp-tongued boss.

Nor, she reminded herself reluctantly, did it allow her to let herself fall for a dark, dour man who was involved with that woman to the extent that he opened his home to her for long periods of time.

Office work or no office work, Emma found herself facing a mound of suds and a stack of dirty dishes after dinner. Dennis was making engine noises on the floor of the dining room as she passed back and forth carrying the dishes into the kitchen. Dan and Margo had disappeared into the room she had come to think of as Dan's office, although it was the one room in the house she had never entered. No one had exactly asked her to clear away, but she couldn't see Margo putting herself out and she knew from experience what sort of a job Dan and Dennis would have done of it.

No, if she were going to be living here for the next few weeks she may as well get used to the idea that typing would be only one of her duties. She might spend several hours a day transcribing tapes and getting out letters, but until Martha came back she strongly suspected she'd be chief cook and bottle washer and heaven knows what else! And if after all that her employer still thought she was getting ideas above her station, she'd probably be conscripted to change the oil and wax the cars!

In the days that followed Dennis became her closest companion, Margo her harshest taskmistress, and Dan . . .

Dan. There was the mystery. After those first days when she had gradually broken through the stern mask of reserve to discover a warm, witty friendliness and a spark of . . . dare she call it interest? . . . there had been a sealing off of the tentative relationship and now she was offered only a cool politeness. Dan never had more to say to her than was necessitated by their living in the same house and Emma tried to subdue the puzzled hurt at his impersonal manner.

There were no more casual, informal meals in the kitchen. Dinner was prepared each night by Dan and herself under the watchful intimidation of Margo as she leaned back and sipped a tall drink and was served in the handsome dining room to the tune of Margo's exploits in search of sensational interviews. There was a good deal of reminiscing between the two of them, and it was all too obvious that they went back a long way. Dennis and Emma were definitely excess baggage. Then the two of them began taking al fresco meals on the porch or even down by the creek under the shade of a squatty, wind-sculpted scrub oak.

By the end of the first week Emma was doing as much housework as office work. At the end of the second, she made a discovery—as long as she took Dennis out of the house and kept up with the chores, Margo didn't care whether or not the transcribing and letters got done. Emma began to suspect that there was nothing very pressing about her office duties and it came to her gradually that housekeeping and baby-sitting were exactly what she had been hired for.

Then why had Rosie Fischer been sent for specifically? Rosie, with her plain, earnest little face and her quick, retentive mind was certainly no better at such chores than anyone else. Fragments of things she had heard about Margo returned to her—that the entourage that followed Margo over the globe was composed almost entirely of men and the few women the star allowed in close quarters with her were over forty, and the plainer, the better.

But surely, Emma thought with a rueful

smile, *she* wouldn't be considered competition! The runt of the litter? The ruffled banty? Oh, she wasn't all that bad; Derek Villers and a few other men in her past wouldn't have made such nuisances of themselves if she had been a hopeless washout. But she was certainly not in the same league with Margo Summerlin, who was easily the most beautiful woman in the news field.

Oh, well—two weeks had gone by and she was due to be paid, a check she would endorse and promptly forward to Hugh. It might be better to repay Derek directly than to give Hugh the chance to blow another lot on the tables, but she couldn't bring herself to do it. Two weeks gone, four to go, and then she'd be well out of it, having acquired a new crop of freckles, a becoming tan, and a hearty disenchantment with television stars of the Summerlin variety.

As well as a perfectly ridiculous infatuation for a man who was already spoken for. You'd think that at twenty-four she'd be past such juvenile attachments, but then, she had never been exposed to a man of Dan's caliber before.

It would pass. Her tan would fade, her new freckles settle in with the perennials, and she would forget what it was like to awaken each day to the feel of a soft salt breeze caressing her. Exhaust fumes and traffic noises would be the rule of the day and she would simply put out of her mind each morning's anticipation of the afternoon spent at the beach with Dennis.

Scanning the last letter—a confirmation of a speaking date some seven months hence—Emma probed under her desk for her platform sandals and turned to greet her employer. Margo strode mannishly into the room to drop down at the larger of the two desks, her lean figure looking anything but mannish in the usual white trousers, this time sparked by a yellow rope belt.

"I'm going to run to the post office for stamps before it closes. These three letters are ready to go if you'll sign them. And . . . "—Emma hesitated to bring up the subject of her pay, but if she didn't, she'd be willing to bet the other woman wouldn't—"if you don't mind, I'd like to have my salary so I can send it to . . ." She looked down at the small stack of letters she was nervously realigning. It was none of Margo's business where she planned to send her check.

"That's all you girls think of, isn't it? Money! If it's not money, it's men!" Margo snapped.

Stung into unwise retaliation, Emma sat up straighter. "Well, I usually get paid for my work. Don't you?"

"Don't get smart with me, Tamplin! You're not the greatest secretary in the business, you know. If you don't like it here, feel free to take off."

"I'm perfectly well satisfied, Miss Summerlin," Emma lied calmly, refusing to be stung into quitting. That would suit Margo Summerlin just fine; she'd consider herself justified in withholding Emma's paycheck in lieu of notice, probably.

She waited silently, a glint of determination in her tilted green eyes as she studied the averted profile. There was no denying her beauty, all right—the cameras didn't lie about that, but they failed to portray the not-so-beautiful disposition that went with those sleek, blond looks. To Emma's way of thinking beauty alone—even beauty allied with brains—didn't make up for a lack of common human decency.

"Oh, all right!" Margo exclaimed impatiently, swinging around to fish her checkbook from the drawer she kept locked in her desk. She dashed off the check, adding her illegible signature to the bottom, and tossed it across to where Emma sat before stalking across the room.

Just before she reached the door, Emma stopped her. "Miss Summerlin, I was given to understand the salary would be almost twice this amount, or is this for one week only?"

Margo spun around and leveled a narrow look of dislike at her. "Your hours aren't exactly nine to five, Tamplin. You can't expect room, board, and every afternoon off to go to the beach for what you're asking."

Emma stood her ground. "Rosie told me what you offered for the six-week term, Miss Summerlin. I came here expecting the same amount —otherwise I'd have stayed home."

"Then ask Mr. Slater to subsidize you. What you do in your spare time around here has nothing to do with me and if you expect me to pay you for baby-sitting the brat, you can think again." So saying, she slammed the door behind her, leaving Emma with her fists and teeth clenched and her eyes closed in pure frustration.

It was true her real duties as a secretary didn't take up very many hours of the day and most of her time was spent in household chores for the absent Martha, as well as in playing with Den-

nis, but it hadn't occurred to her that she
wouldn't be paid her full salary. She could ill
afford a vacation at half pay now, of all times—
not with Hugh and Derek weighing so heavily on
her mind. She had had a call from her brother
just two nights before and he had told her he was
still doing part-time bookkeeping at the club to
help pay off his tab. But if Emma knew Hugh, it
was like taking on an alcoholic as a bartender,
and she had hung up in despair. It was bad
enough to tread water, but sometimes she felt as
if she were swimming against an outgoing tide
and getting further from the shore all the time.

She simply had to get enough to pay off that
dreadful man. Then she and Hugh would move
to another area and start off fresh. Her own
skills would be in demand most anywhere; it
was Hugh who mattered now. Her father had
almost ruined his life with gambling. Emma's
mother had left him just a few months before
she had been killed in a hotel fire and the shock
had seemed to straighten Ed Tamplin out. When
he remarried, Treva, Hugh's mother, had kept
him on such a tight rein that he had neither time
nor money to throw away on gambling, even if
the inclination still remained. If she had also
managed to wean him from his daughter, and
her own son to boot, then that was their business. It had had the effect of drawing Hugh and
Emma closer together at a time when Emma
could appreciate a brother almost her own age.
Hugh fluctuated from the protective attitude of
an older brother to the dependence of a younger
one, a little weak but genuinely fond of his
adopted sister.

With a sigh, she left the room and wandered off in search of Dennis to see if he wanted to go with her. A trip to the post office might keep her occupied for a few minutes, but she felt in need of something that would totally exhaust her so that she could sleep tonight instead of mulling over a troublesome situation. Maybe with a fresh outlook in the morning she could come up with the best course to take. Somehow it seemed anticlimactic to go trailing back to Washington with a job half done—whatever the job was.

She didn't allow herself to dwell on the real reason for her reluctance to leave the island.

Chapter Three

One glance through the kitchen door was enough to reveal that Dennis was proudly demonstrating his Polaroid camera to several boys from Avon. It had been a parting gift from his parents before they went to Europe and Dennis had delighted in catching Emma and Dan off guard. He had shot Dan glowering, with a pencil in his tccth and his hair standing on end, but his favorite shot was of Emma in her bathrobe, with a towel draped around her head. She was pointing a finger at him, chastising him for invading her privacy. Mad as a wet hen, Dan had remarked when the delighted boy had showed it to him. Not a banty hen, at least, for her feathers had been too wet to be ruffled. Oddly enough, Dennis never took any of Margo. With a real, live celebrity in the house you'd think he'd be trading pictures of her like baseball cards.

The heat outdoors hit her a solid blow as she sidled gingerly onto the hot plastic seat of her car and shoved the letters onto the dashboard. She had written Hugh a note apologizing for the fact that the check was smaller than she had led him to expect and she wondered again if she wouldn't be smart to simply cut her losses and return to Washington, hoping for an immediate assignment. True, her rates were smaller there, especially as the agency collected a commission and she had her living expenses as well. Rosie's sister was sharing the apartment for the time being, but they could double up if necessary.

Oh, bother! Why couldn't things go as planned for once? This could have been the perfect vacation break, for working on assignment, as she did, there were no paid vacations. She had not been able to afford a real break for three years, other than an occasional weekend.

Letters mailed, stamps already sticking together in the humid warmth of her purse, she swatted a greenhead, started her car, and drove back to the Ridge, parking in the hot shade of a grove of small bay trees.

Dan greeted her from the screened porch with an invitation that halted her in her steps, coming as it did after almost two weeks of cool, perfunctory politeness. "How about a swim, Emma?"

Cautiously, she replied that she usually took a dip in the afternoons, a fact which he well knew, for he had given permission for Dennis to accompany her the first few times. Margo had persuaded him that it was good for both Emma and Dennis to have someone to swim with and it had quickly become a habit.

"Dennis tells me you're having trouble getting the hang of body surfing. The tide's about right for it now, so what do you say we give it a go in about . . . five minutes?"

Breathless at the idea of sharing anything with Dan Slater, Emma nodded and hurried away to tug her brown jersey one-piece suit on over her damp body. She didn't ask whether or not Margo and Dennis would be accompanying them, fearful of breaking the spell. It was the first time he had volunteered to spend any time in her company since Margo had returned and Emma knew Dennis missed the easy camaraderie he had shared with his uncle as well. The net had been brought in and stored and there were no more filthy, tiring, exciting expeditions out to the fishing grounds. No more horseplay with the garden hose, either.

"Ready? Good! Wear something on your feet, and please, not those stilts you run around here on." His opaque eyes seemed to touch all parts of her body without once leaving her face. She decided it was an optical illusion.

Her own eyes were having a hard enough time staying away from the spendid physique revealed by the brief white trunks he wore, and when he stepped into a pair of thick leather sandals he grinned at her. "There was a time, believe it or not, when I could carve my initials on the soles of my feet. That was before too much city living softened me up, though."

Following two paces behind his longer stride

as they headed down the driveway, Emma concluded that if city living had softened him up
anywhere, it was somewhere that didn't show.
What she could see above and below the band of
white was hard, brown, and lean.

They paused at the edge of the asphalt highway and Emma felt a strange sense of isolation
for a moment as she stared at the heat-induced
mirages on either side of them. It was as if they
were suspended in space . . . or alone on an
island. I should be so lucky, she thought derisively, dancing along after him over the hot
sand.

The color of the water was between emerald
and sapphire, with cool blue-white lacings
where the breakers began several hundred feet
out from the shore. The ever present salt haze
that hovered just above the surf in both directions made distant swimmers and surf fishermen look as if they were floating in a fog. Emma
was selfishly glad that they had this stretch of
beach to themselves, at least for the time being.
She still didn't know where Margo and Dennis
were and she wasn't going to spoil her own fun
by asking.

"How strong a swimmer are you?" Dan asked
as they shucked their sandals and dropped their
towels on the hard-packed sand.

"Fair to middling. I can do quite a few lengths
of the pool, but I haven't had all that much
experience in the ocean. None at all, in fact,"
she confessed, "until I came down here."

"Good Lord, that hadn't occurred to me when I
sent you and the boy off here every afternoon."
His expression was more exasperation with him-

self than anger with her, Emma was glad to see.
She assured him that they mostly played around
in the shallows if there were no other swimmers, trying to ride the waves only from a few
yards out.

"All the same, don't come again unless I'm
free to come with you."

"And that won't be very often," she retorted,
miffed at his lack of faith in her ability to look
after his nephew. "I do have sense enough not to
let him get into trouble."

"Famous last words. You'd be in over your
head almost as soon as Dennis was, half-pint,
but forget it for now. I'll see that you get your
swimming time in, but from now on you'll have
to put up with my company as well as Dennis's."

Unwilling to admit to herself the cause of the
fluttering hollow that opened up in her midsection at his words, Emma raced to the water and
floundered out through the suds to dive beneath
an incoming wave. She came up several seconds
later, wiping the brine from her eyes, to see
Dan's dark head and shoulders ahead of her. He
was laughing when he turned to wave her on
out.

"Come on, there's no current at all today so
we'll swim out to the bar and catch an express."

She set to in her best YWCA style and Dan
obviously held back so as not to outdistance her
by too many lengths. When he turned to her
again and told her to stand up, she obeyed him
blindly, only to have a wave break over her head
in a cascade of crystal green. Flailing wildly,
she came up sputtering, and Dan lifted her up by
the waist and grinned down at her.

"I forget what a shrimp you are." He held her off when she swung a playful fist at him. "All right, all right, a miniature! I'd better hang on to you, but when I tell you to go, start swimming for shore as hard as you can. When you feel the power of the wave take over, stiffen out and ride it on in. Got it?"

"If you say so," she answered doubtfully, far more conscious of the warmth of his hands in the cool water than the instructions he imparted. For once she was glad of her size; it had its benefits after all.

She managed the first one beautifully, washing up in the rough gravel of the surf with a painful force. She stood eagerly, regained her balance, and plowed back out through the breakers, ready to try again. It had been the most exhilarating experience of her life, being pushed along by tons of rushing water—like nothing she had ever felt before—and she couldn't wait to do it again.

Dan met her halfway and swam beside her, reaching out to support her once they gained the sandy bar offshore, but this time she just seemed to drop through the slope of the racing wave with an anticlimactic helplessness.

"What went wrong?" she called out plaintively, treading water and looking apprehensively over her shoulder to where still another of the huge combers was piling up toward them.

"Happens like that sometimes. A matter of timing, usually. Never mind, you'll get the next one. Here it is, so get ready!" He hauled her close to him and supported her with a hand under her stomach. There was nothing at all personal in his touch. All the same, Emma found it awfully hard to keep her mind on what she was doing when he launched her and took off beside her, swimming for all he was worth.

She rode the next three and then insisted on treading water and getting on the next one all by herself. It proved disastrous. It was all right for the first few seconds but then, when it began to break early, Emma was caught beneath the hollow curl and thrown under by a back-breaking force. The next few moments were among the most frightening she had ever undergone. Tons of churning, sandy water beat her down again and again, dragging her along the bottom as if it would never release her. Her lungs were bursting, shells were scouring her skin, and her limbs were tossed around like matchsticks. When, by some fluke, she regained her feet for an instant and managed a gasp of air, she was struck in the back and swept under by still another wave.

This time, though, Dan had located her. He grabbed her arm and held on with a strength that threatened to dislocate her shoulder, dragging her up against his hard body to shield her from the surging, waist-deep waters, and she clung to him desperately.

"Sorry, honey," Dan managed to pant. "You really took a momicking that time, didn't you?"

"Whatever it is, I took it," she gasped breathlessly, resting her head on his rough chest as he waded ashore with her in his arms.

"We'll sit out the next few while you get yourself sorted out, shall we? In fact, I expect you've had enough for today." He put her gently on the sand and eased himself down beside her, picking up a towel to dry her face.

To winded to protest, Emma allowed him to stroke her face dry and rub her dripping hair. The gentleness of his strength, a gentleness she had previously seen him extend only to his young nephew, for some strange reason brought tears to the surface of her eyes.

Or it could have been the salt. She said as much when Dan tipped her face up to study it with those disconcerting eyes of his.

"A tumble like that can be pretty upsetting," he told her, using the corner of the towel to catch a tear that trickled down her sandy cheek. He blotted it so tenderly that she didn't even feel the grains and when he smiled down at her it was as if the sun had broken through storm clouds. Her heart did all sorts of acrobatics and she took a deep, shaky breath and jumped to her feet.

"I want to catch just one more good one before I go home," she called out, racing down toward the water as his protest followed her. She had always heard that when you got thrown the best thing to do was to remount and try again and that was exactly why she was so anxious to get back out to deep water and climb aboard the biggest wave she could find. It had nothing at all to do with the perilous effect Dan's nearness had on her in her weakened condition, she told herself sternly.

Dan rode beside her, watching carefully, but he didn't touch her again, not even when they finally gave up and waded laughingly ashore, braced and stimulated by the cool, briny surf. He handed her a towel and tossed his own around his neck, picking up both pairs of sandals in one hand and leading the way to the line of dunes.

"Sand's cooled off by now," he promised her, and she found it to be true.

At the crest of the dunes they paused as if by unspoken consent. From here they could look down on the several random wings of Larkin's Ridge against the somber greenery that surrounded it. Emma had learned that the odd design was intended to allow whatever breeze there was free access to all parts of the house and it worked, being cool on all but the hottest days.

Behind lay the bright finger of water that led out to the reflected opalescence of the Sound. The small boats moored there that were so blindingly white in the noonday blueness appeared now as misty silhouettes. To the right, the village of Avon—or Kinnakeet, as Dennis called it—nestled in the dark green of cedars, yaupons, and stunted live oaks. It was a scattering of white houses seemingly dropped in a random pattern that tapered off into clusters of beach cottages on all sides. Church steeple and water tower broke the low horizon and all was shrouded in the ever-present salt haze that seemed to Emma to descend each day at dusk.

Hatteras was lost in the distance as the orange sun sank lower in the sky and the villages of Frisco and Buxton emerged as low smudges against the blinding surface of the water. Emma looked over her shoulder at the ocean and back again at the Sound. "I never quite realized before just how tiny the island is," she murmured, caught up in a feeling of precariousness as she saw the wide, shallow Pamlico and the vast Atlantic separated by only a fragile, thread-like barrier of sand.

"It's been here a long time," Dan told her. "The Indians lived in several villages on the Sound side before the first white man ever set foot on these shores. Matter of fact, their blood-line was probably well diluted by all the seamen who made it ashore when their ships foundered on Diamond Shoals . . . not to mention by the so-called Lost Colonists."

Emma sent him a questioning glance. "You think they came here to the Outer Banks?" she asked as they resumed their slow way down the inside of the dunes.

Dan's solid, muscular shoulders lifted and fell expressively as he guided her past a clump of sand spurs. "Logic says so. It was where they said they were going. Croatan, it was called on the early maps—what was the lower part of this island and the upper part of Ocracoke island. Since the only Indians remaining friendly to them were here and they said they were going here, it's logical to assume they did. Especially since the next person to search the area for them found Hatorask Indians living here who said their ancestors could speak from a book. That was John Lawson, about a hundred years later, and he found Indians here with auburn hair—like yours, maybe—and with gray and blue eyes. He said they valued themselves greatly for their affinity with the English."

"What does that mean?" Emma prompted

him, delighted at this slightly professorial side to the complex man beside her.

Dan took her arm and hurried her across the soft asphalt. "It means that the melting pot started here," he told her with a slanting grin. "And we'd better get a move on, because I don't know about you, but I'm starved. I expect Margo's back by now, too."

"I mostly feel waterlogged," Emma admitted, fighting off the feeling of letdown that the mention of Margo brought on.

"You'll be sore as the dickens tomorrow, but if you're game, we'll try it again."

On the verge of making a silly remark about seeking Margo's permission, she thought better of it and was glad she had when the blond appeared in the front door. Her narrow, pale eyes went from one of them to the other and her expression wasn't precisely welcoming.

"It looks as if you two have had a whale of a good time," she remarked tartly.

"We have," Dan answered her easily, opening the door and allowing Emma to go first.

Margo had stepped back at their approach and now Emma was forced to run the gamut of her accusing stare. "I thought you were going to mail my letters," she said with a sniff. "I particularly wanted them to get off today!"

"Since you hadn't signed them and the mail had already gone for the day, I didn't think it would matter. I'll mail them first thing in the morning," Emma promised her evenly, fighting to keep her temper.

"You'll mail them tonight! Who knows where

you'll go haring off to tomorrow! The boy is in the kitchen wanting something to eat and I'm getting pretty tired of waiting myself, Dan." She turned to the man who stood waiting with what Emma considered admirable patience for the tirade to end. "Why don't we go out to that place that has such good stuffed flounder? There's no point in steaming up the house when we have a first-rate restaurant close by."

Nodding briefly, Dan agreed. "Suits me. Emma? How long will it take you to get ready?"

"Oh, but . . ." Margo began, when Dan strode across the living room and called out for his nephew.

"Dennis? Hop to it! We're dining out tonight, so see to it you wear shoes for a change or you'll eat out back with the cats."

It was perfectly obvious to Emma what Margo thought of his plans to make their outing a foursome and for the life of her she couldn't fathom Dan's intent, but far be it from her to miss all the fun. The glow inside her at the knowledge that Dan wanted her along more than made up for any sticks and stones Margo might cast.

Ten minutes later, Emma emerged wearing a white cotton sleeveless dress, her coral necklace repeated in the color of her platform sandals. Her hair was twisted in a damp knot on top of her head, the tangles brushed over hastily in her impatience.

Dennis was waiting outside her bedroom door, looking unnaturally clean in spite of the fact that his shirttail was out and his shoes not properly tied. He gave her a surprisingly unchildlike grin, a conspiratorial wink, and when she asked if he were ready, he held out his hands for her inspection. "We went swimming in the Sound, Elmo, Chuck, and me, and Elmo's daddy was there to keep an eye on us, so don't worry."

Emma and Dennis took the back seat, of course. This time, instead of the jeep, they were in the dark blue Audi Dan kept garaged beside Margo's sports car against the deleterious effects of the atmosphere. She found herself studying the set of Dan's well-shaped head on his bronzed neck above the white knit shirt and it occurred to her that he could have been an athlete. For that matter, he might well be, for he didn't live here on the island all year around. So far she had not found the nerve to ask pointblank what he did for a living, and since he was not a man to talk about himself, she was no wiser than she had been two weeks ago.

Dinner was an unqualified success, especially as Margo's attempts to corral all Dan's attention for herself were thwarted from the very first when they were hailed by a Slater-dark man of some fifty years or so and his party. After a spate of introductions, the table was extended and then they were eight!

Field Slater was indeed Dan's cousin, as Emma had immediately suspected. The wife of the other man was another cousin—more distant, Emma found, as they laughingly explained the begats to her. All four of the newcomers knew Margo and Emma felt a twinge of something unworthy as she was reminded again of how closely interwoven were the lives of Dan and Margo.

But whereas most nights she retired to her room to the disturbing sounds of those two voices discussing, even arguing about people, places, and events she knew little of, tonight Emma found herself quickly swept into the conversation. Dennis was included, and although there was no conscious effort, as far as Emma could see, to exclude Margo, somehow the talk seemed to swirl around the table without much more than an occasional acid rejoinder from the coolly sophisticated blond.

One rowdy tale followed another as the group dug into enormous seafood platters and Emma was fascinated to see a subtle change come over Dan. His accent, that tantalizing hint of brogue with roots that struck directly back to Walter Raleigh's England, became more pronounced as he reminisced with his cousins over pranks that had Dennis's eyes sparkling.

"Yeah, back when I was a boy there weren't no law on the island," Field said. He pronounced it oiland, as did many of the natives Emma had talked to. "Didn't have to have licenses then— not for you nor your car, either—and many's the time we went firelighting Trent Woods for deer from the fenders of that old Ford."

"To hear them talk of it, you'd think they were the good old days, but let me tell you, when the freight boat came once or twice a week from Elizabeth City, and that was the only time you got meat or cow's milk, why, they weren't so good." Field's wife, a dark-haired woman whose startlingly blue eyes lent her an unusual sort of beauty, went on to remind the men that there was seldom a doctor available on the islands in those days, either. "Why, my mother said she nursed me through scarlet fever thinking it weren't nothing but a bad case o' sunburn and the flu," she laughed. "Midwife come to deliver Nathan an' said, 'Law, Miz Sal, that youngun's had the scarlet fever.' Ma told her she did think I was peelin' funny."

The laughter was general and carried into further reminiscences. It was while they were talking of the days when the only phones on the island were in the Coast Guard stations and the weather bureau that Margo stubbed her cigarette out in her plate and interrupted.

"I forgot to mention it, Emma," she said coolly, the light from the ship's lantern turning her pale hair into a sleek cap of gold. "There was a call for you this afternoon. Your boyfriend, Derek something or other. Wasn't too happy at missing you, but he said to tell you he'd be seeing you before long."

The party broke up shortly after that. None of the others could have had any idea of the wave of despair that washed over Emma at Margo's casually imparted information, but something seemed to go out of the evening after that. Field said he had to be up before the heat of day to work on his boat and his wife, Mary, teased him about it.

While the men argued good-naturedly over the check—with Dan winning the doubtful honor of picking up the tab for a dinner for eight—Mary told the others about her husband's new boat. It

was a fiberglass convertible sports fisherman
that was supposed to be practically main-
tenance free—or so he had rationalized when he
bought it. Since then, if she wanted to see him
she had to go down to the slip behind the house
where he kept his fleet moored. "That makes
four now, including the flat and the dory, and if
you ask me, that's responsibility enough for any
man!"

Her husband came up behind her and slipped
a large work-roughened hand under her elbow.
"You tryin' to limit the size of the family now,
honey? I was plannin' on at least a couple
more," he said, grinning. "Say, how about we go
out for a day o' clamming, crabbing, fishing, and
whatever else we can get up to come Sunday.
What say, young Dennis—how's it strike you?"

It was quickly agreed on as they filed out of the
air-conditioned restaurant into the warm, fragrant darkness, with Dennis making plans to
include his young pals from the village and
Margo expressively silent. Emma was silent,
too, but only because she was feeling almost sick
at the conflicting emotions that churned turbu-
lently through her. Derek again.

Derek Villers—it seemed she couldn't get far
enough away from the man! On the other hand,
there was Dan, and today, and the promise of
Sunday.

By the time they reached Larkin's Ridge Dennis was asleep against her arm, and when Dan
reached in the dark back seat to lift him out,
Emma felt the shaft of his eyes piercing her
precarious composure.

"All right with you about Sunday?" he asked.

"Oh . . . yes, fine. I'm looking forward to it,"
she replied distractedly.

"Who's Derek?"

She took a deep breath and swallowed it,
edging out of the car and feeling her skirt stick
to the back of her thighs in the oppressive heat.
"Derek? Oh . . . just somebody I knew back in
Washington," she replied when Dan seemed determined to wait for her answer. He stood there,
the boy hanging limply in his arms, and waited
while she went before him up the steps and held
the door open for him. Margo had gone on ahead
and Emma could hear her at the liquor cabinet
now.

"What's between you?"

Stunned at his temerity, Emma could only
stare at him. "It's none of your business," she
declared finally.

"You're right," he said shortly, striding away
toward the boy's bedroom.

Emma stared helplessly after the white-clad
figure as it faded into the darkness of the back
hallway, turning into the open door. How totally
unlike Dan to even ask such a personal question,
and how achingly she longed to be able to pour
out the whole story to him. Seeing the strong
arms supporting so firmly, yet so gently, the
small, sleeping boy, Emma felt a wrench somewhere inside her that was an actual physical
pain. She turned and went to her own room and
shut the door, unwilling to be there when Dan
emerged from putting Dennis to bed.

Sometime during the night, the breeze
dropped, leaving behind a sultry stillness that

droned with insect life. The first thought that
filtered into Emma's head was the outing on
Sunday and she wondered why she should have
such a forboding feeling. Then, as she lifted the
hair from her damp neck and pulled her nightgown from her sticky body, she remembered—
Derek had said he'd see her soon.

Oh, dear, she thought impatiently. She
snapped on the overhead fan, wishing she had
left it on when she had gone to bed last night
instead of counting on the fitful breeze. By the
time she had showered and dressed in white
shorts and a loose-fitting shirt that had belonged
to Hugh she had managed to convince herself
that Derek was referring to the time when she'd
be done with this job. He *had* to mean that!

Sounds of the awakening household greeted
her; Dan's electric shaver and Dennis's drawers being jerked open and rumpled through.
Margo's shower alerted her to the fact that there
was coffee to be made and she set to with
something almost resembling amusement. A
great deal had come clear lately. Most of it
related to the fact that when Dan's housekeeper
left the day after Margo's arrival the tempera-
mental star had found herself in a predicament;
with typical chauvinism, Dan and Dennis just
assumed that a woman in the house meant that
certain chores would get themselves done.

Serving up bacon, scrambled eggs, toast, and
coffee, Emma munched on a piece of toast as
she cleared away the utensils. The table held
four, but she found it was easier in the long run
to serve the others and eat when she could
herself. It surprised her to find Margo an early

riser, but she still didn't risk the other woman's uncertain disposition until after the third cup of coffee.

"Have you any letters to get off this morning?" she asked now. "Or shall I get the laundry on the line? I think we're in for some showers later on."

"Cultivating a fisherman's weather eye?" Dan jibed easily, draining the last of the coffee from the pot.

"Wishful thinking," she told him.

"Do the laundry, by all means, and don't forget to collect the things from my room. Oh, and when you go to the post office, go by the store and see if you can get . . . here, I'll write you out a list."

So I won't forget, Emma thought irritably as Margo turned to tell Dan that she was thinking of inviting some people over for drinks soon.

"If you mean Field and Mary and the Hardys, they'd prefer dinner."

"Actually, I was talking about the Halperns. Remember, he was involved in that mess in Houston last month? Well, I happen to know that there's a quiet little hideaway here on the island where people of that level come to get away from it all, *and* I happen to know that Ross and Ava Halpern will be in residence from the sixteenth to the twenty-third. I think over a few friendly drinks in a nice, relaxed setting I just might persuade Ross to give me an interview— what do you think?" The whole time Margo had been speaking Emma had been aware of a difference in her and it finally dawned on her that she was hearing the studio voice. Lower, huskier, with a wider range, it was entirely different from the normal tones of the woman who ordered the household.

"I think you'd better not touch it," Dan replied calmly.

The professional voice was gone as Margo's head was flung up. In flattened tones she demanded to know what he meant. "It's my job to see that the taxpayers know what's going on and I know a lot more than they do about it!"

"You know what your private sources have fed you, but you don't know why that particular angle was leaked, nor do you know what special interests would be served by publicizing it. Leave it, Margo," Dan ordered, rising from the table.

"Oh, no! You run your rag and let me handle my own show! You're jealous—you've always been jealous because I've scooped you on so many stories—but I never expected you to be small about it."

Dennis had wiped his mouth hastily and inexpertly and escaped through the back door and Emma, in the middle of washing the dishes, was about to follow when Dan's next words caught her up short.

"Since Margo doesn't need your services this morning, Emma," he began with deceptive mildness, when Margo interrupted.

"I didn't say that! I told her to do the laundry and go to the grocers and then I'd decide whether or not I needed her questionable skills as a typist!"

A wave of embarrassment washed over Emma, leaving behind a feeling of helplessness. She felt like a bone being fought over by two dogs, neither of whom really wanted it. She was on the verge of throwing down her towel and walking out permanently when she was halted once more.

In a voice that should have warned them both, Dan said, "Then I take it you can do without the questionable services altogether?"

"You're absolutely right I can!" Margo pounced. "There's got to be somebody on this benighted island who can wipe off a dish and put a decent meal on the table. As for secretarial work, I'd do better to hire *you* than to try to make do with someone who's never around when I need her!"

While Emma bristled at this unfair allegation, her misery forgotten under a surge of righteous indignation, Dan nailed Margo to the wall with the force of his narrowed black eyes.

"First, Margo," he said evenly, "you haven't the resources to hire me, and secondly, when you invited yourself to spend the summer here, we both know why I agreed. At least, I *thought* I knew. Now I'm beginning to wonder. At any rate," he continued, holding them both immobile by the sheer power of his personality, "I'll take you at your word and relieve you of Miss Tamplin's services, because it happens that I do need her—and in a secretarial capacity—not as a maid of all work."

The two women stood transfixed for several seconds. Then Margo, whose mouth had dropped open, snapped it closed and glared malevolently at Emma. "Don't tell me you've opened a branch office, darling. No! You're going to write the great American novel, aren't you? But then, all newspaper editors are frustrated novelists, aren't they?"

Confused, Emma looked imploringly from one to the other, and then it occurred to her that Margo wasn't speaking to her but to Dan. A newspaper editor? A novelist? Things were spinning too fast and she was beginning to get dizzy!

"Forget the dishes, Emma," Dan ordered peremptorily. "Margo was right about one thing, at least. There is someone who can come to wipe off a dish and put a meal on the table, so you're both relieved on that score. And for laughs, Margo, it *is* the great American novel . . . quote, end quote." He turned to Emma and there was a softening of his implacable jaw, a relaxing of the grim lines beside his mouth. "Emma, I'll be needing you from nine to eleven and again after four. If I decide to work some at night, will you be available?"

Margo chimed in sweetly, "Oh, she'll be available, all right. Her type always is."

Chapter Four

The outraged rebuttal went unmade as Emma watched Margo stride from the room. With the light of battle in her eyes, Emma actually took a step to follow when Dan touched her arm and smiled, shaking his head slowly at her. "Hold off until you cool down, Emma. Margo's an old pro when it comes to verbal warfare, and in spite of that touch of red in your hair, you're no match for her. Besides, believe it or not, she's not as bad as she paints herself."

Emma chose not to, but she swallowed her anger and followed Dan to his office, casting a guilty look over her shoulder at the half-finished dishes in the cooling suds.

Two hours and one phone call later she returned for iced coffee to find the kitchen sparkling and a line of laundry hanging limply under a brazen sky. Dennis was down by the water with two other boys and sitting in the shade of the largest of the scrub oaks was a woman Emma recalled seeing around the village, her fingers agilely snapping beans as she kept an eye on the trio.

Balancing the two tall glasses on a tray, she returned to the room that was more a study than an office. She felt as if she were a different person from the distraught girl who had followed Dan Slater as he strode into the attractive room a couple of hours earlier.

For one thing, she knew who she was working for now. No more of the ambivalent swinging back and forth between the two roles. She had spent the morning transcribing page after page of scrawled notes for the man who was editor-in-chief of one of the capital's most astute newspapers, a small daily dedicated to analysis of the political climate. It wasn't the sort of paper she read very often herself, and when she did, she understood little of it, but she was well aware of the high esteem in which it was held by both the business and political communities.

Her work, however, was concerned with the book Dan was working on—not the great American novel he had claimed, but a biography of a man Emma had never heard of until that morning. She had her first taste of research when Dan told her what he was searching for and turned over to her reams of fine print on early patents dealing with communications.

The coffee finished, Emma sat her sweating glass back on the tray and prepared to get back to work when Dan surprised her with the suggestion that they take a swimming break. "We both need to get our circulation going again and then we'll have lunch and pick up again when it cools off a little, maybe with that rain you predicted."

Emma couldn't very well tell him that her circulation was going full blast, thank you, after two hours of sitting across the desk from him, hearing that deeply attractive voice and watching his square, well-kept hands as they shuffled through pages and pages of the all-but-illegible script. It was pure hero worship, infatuation of the most juvenile kind, she chided herself, remembering how her pulses had set a new record the last time she had felt his hands on her body as he dragged her ashore.

Since then—and before then, for that matter— he had treated her with a cool, impersonal sort of friendliness, as if she were a pal of Dennis's. She pushed aside the few puzzling instances of something more intimate, for they were no more than any man would allot a personable female. If he wanted a secretary, then she'd be the best darned secretary he ever had, and if he wanted a surfing companion, then she'd do her best to keep up with him. Surely there was no danger in such a deliberately unemotional approach. Surely if she made up her mind to look but not touch she'd be safe.

Margo had taken off earlier in her racy red sports car and Dennis was eating gingerbread in the kitchen when Emma sought him out to see if he wanted to go to the beach. She introduced herself to Salina Pugh and said they'd be back for lunch about one thirty after Dennis informed her that he was going clamming with the two Pugh boys.

"Count on clam strips and maybe fritters, too, for supper, Emma," he told her confidently, and Emma told him she could hardly wait.

The surf was completely different today. Despite the total lack of wind, it was gray and rough and more than a little intimidating, although Dan seemed to greet the change eagerly. "Storm offshore," he told her. "We're edging into the hurricane season now and there might be more of a current today, but we'll get some great rides in if you're game."

If he'd tried deliberately, he couldn't have come up with a better way to spur her on, and Emma ran out into the frothing surf, flinching at the unexpected coolness but plunging on to dive under a crashing breaker.

It was rough! There wasn't all that much current, but the lack of orderliness confused her and she found she had to keep on her toes, both figuratively and literally, so as not to be swamped.

They rode the first few together, with Dan's powerful form right beside her, and they washed up on the beach laughing, feeling the scrape of hard-packed sand on bare skin and finding it not unpleasant.

"You can bail out before you run aground if you'd rather, but you'd probably get knocked off your pins if you did," he told her, but Emma didn't want to relinquish a single foot of the thrilling ride. All that unleashed power carrying her before it was a little like being on a giant roller coaster and she continued to let herself go until she ran aground, collecting a suit full of sand and a skin full of abrasions.

Each time she scrambled to her feet, laughing exultantly, and waded out again to wait for the next one. Dan, although he had little more to say and touched her not at all, kept a constant eye on the small figure in the brown suit.

By the time they headed home again, Emma knew why Dan insisted on taking a rest after lunch. She was asleep on her feet, drugged with the weight of her own body after the buoyancy of the sea, and it was all she could do to get through lunch without toppling over asleep.

Margo hadn't returned and Dennis was eating a picnic lunch with the Pugh boys down at the edge of the water, plotting another clamming trip after the abortive attempt of the morning, according to Mrs. Pugh. Dan sat across the kitchen table from Emma and grinned openly at her feeble efforts to hold her eyes open.

"Come on, you take the hammock and I'll take the lounger," he offered, leading her to the side porch.

She had expected to go to her room and nap and now she turned to him in confusion. "I sleep on my stomach," she said tentatively.

"Then you take the lounger."

"But you want it," she objected.

"It's wide enough for two."

Face flaming, she headed for the hammock, but he stopped her with a word. "Afraid?"

"Of what?" she countered.

"That's what I want to know. All I'm proposing is a short nap. If you settle down in your own bed you'll oversleep and wake up groggy. Here on the porch the household noises will keep you from going under too deeply."

She looked for a flaw in his reasoning, but not very hard. It all sounded so plausible and Emma pushed aside the small voice that told her she could well go under so deeply she might never surface again, but not in the way he meant.

"Why not?" she said, placing a knee on the wide double lounger with its heaps of colorful pillows. All of a sudden it was far too inviting for Emma in her lethargic state to resist.

Before joining her Dan switched on the ceiling fan and its gentle whir aided in blocking out the sounds of cutlery as Mrs. Pugh finished up in the kitchen. A homey sound that made it perfectly acceptable, Emma rationalized sleepily, for her to be contemplating sleeping with her employer on a screened-in porch with the scent of sun-warmed myrtles and oleanders to further seduce her senses.

Cautiously, she edged over as far as she could and averted her face when she felt the cushion give under added weight. She was daft! She was plumb out of her mind even to consider lying down beside him, but there had been nothing at all in his manner to make her think he had in mind more than a nap. He might be settling his nephew down for the afternoon for all the attention he paid her now.

Oh, yeah? her sleepy mind argued. How many bosses have suggested you settle down for an innocent little midday nap with them? And how many would you accept—purely on a platonic basis, of course?

Background noises—the childish voices, the hum of a vacuum cleaner, the ever present sound of the surf that was felt in the bones more than actually heard after the first few days, and the drone of drunken bees lurching away from a lantana outside the porch—all these faded into the distance and she slept. Sometime later consciousness returned slowly and with it the impression of being watched. Her eyelids remained tightly closed at first, heavy with the inertia of sleep, but then it became a defensive mechanism. She could feel Dan's stare, feel his warm breath playing over her newly sensitized skin, and when her lashes quivered with the necessity to be still, he laughed, a low, soft sound that triggered a rise of goose bumps along her arms and thighs.

"How long have you been awake?" he murmured.

"How long have you?" she countered.

"What makes you think I could sleep?"

Her eyes drifted open at that and she turned her head to see him propped up on one elbow, surveying her lazily from a distance of mere inches.

"I want to kiss you, Emma," he told her softly, frankly.

"Why?" She was held captive by the strange, cool fire of his dark eyes.

"The usual reasons, I guess. Why not?"

"You're casual enough about it," Emma retorted, perversely piqued by his offhand manner.

"And you'd prefer more intensity? It's not that

sort of an afternoon, Emma, and not the sort of kiss I had in mind."

Mesmerized, helplessly knowing herself of unsound mind, she whispered, "What sort did you have in mind?"

He showed her. It was a slow, summery sort of kiss, a tentative caress of the lips, a sweet, indolent touching that neither pleaded nor demanded. Her lips remained closed, softened by the touch of his firm, sensuous mouth as he brushed them gently, then allowed the light pressure to grow still until the tension between them was unbearable. His hands had not once touched her, nor did they now; he merely lifted his face and looked intently into her eyes and she saw herself reflected in the dark shadowy pools of his.

"That sort," he murmured, "for starters."

The sound of Margo's car roaring up the driveway broke the spell, but Dan seemed in no hurry to get up. Emma couldn't very well climb over him and she was trapped against the screen until he allowed her to move. The last thing she needed was to be found by her ex-employer like this! Now, more than ever, she needed to know just what was between Dan and Margo, but she could never presume on this one, sweet, quicksilver moment to pry into his personal life. She knew too well the chilling power of those eyes that could warm like glowing coals and freeze even more quickly.

In the silence that followed the screeching halt of Margo's car, the gutsy rumble of thunder was heard from a distance and it seemed almost an outgrowth of her own troubled feelings. She felt as if she were adrift on a rough sea in a leaky intertube, and when Dan finally swung his feet to the floor and turned to give her a hand, she ignored it to scramble across the colorful cushion with more haste than dignity, hurrying in to the safety of her own room.

Dinner that night began with Dennis's excuses for the absence of clams, some of which sounded pretty fanciful, even to Emma's unknowledgeable ears. Margo seemed preoccupied and it wasn't until they were served great slabs of Mrs. Pugh's fig pudding that she brought up the subject on her mind. Pushing aside the untouched pudding—under Dennis's watchful eye, Emma noted with amusement—she lighted up a cigarette and leaned back in her chair, a movement which threw into relief her flawless figure under the light covering of a tailored white silk shirt.

"Halpern has agreed to an interview," she said triumphantly.

A slight tightening of the lips was the only reaction from Dan. He stirred his coffee and carefully placed the antique silver spoon in his saucer.

"Well?" Margo prompted. "Aren't you going to warn me against going off half cocked? You always were an anchor, Dan. If I hadn't listened to you more times than I should have, I'd probably be on a top network by now instead of one that trails in the ratings—except for my own show, that is."

"I thought you were headed for the Persian Gulf pretty soon," Dan sidetracked.

"It's on too short a fuse to suit me. The studio won't send a crew in without enough State Department red tape to hang us all."

"Central America?"

"Same thing. Political dynamite these days."

"That used to be meat and drink to you, Margo. Are you getting timid in your latter years?" Dan taunted gently under Emma's fascinated gaze.

"You can shut up, Dan Slater! I'm no more in my latter years than you are and you can't tell me you consider yourself middle-aged!"

He laughed at that. "My years don't bother me, Margo, and I recall a time when you were anxious to pile on a few more than you could lay claim to. You were, what? About twenty-two, trying hard to make yourself convincing as a neophyte newscaster?"

"Dan Slater, you've known me too long!" Margo declared with a grudging grin that bespoke an intimacy of long standing.

"Not to mention too well," he added laconically.

Again Emma was treated to a sample of the famous Summerlin charm. "Well, you'll have to admit a woman with a few good years to her credit is a sight more interesting than some wide-eyed ingenue. Given the same basic equipment, a woman's mind can spell the difference between boredom and fascination and you were never a man to put up with ennui, were you? Which reminds me," she added smugly, "how's the project coming along? Have you managed to brainwash your little helper about the world's greatest unsung hero?"

"You mentioned brains, Margo," Dan said urbanely. "There's more than one dimension to be considered. There's depth, width, and . . ."

"And thickness," Margo jibed, stabbing out her cigarette in the untouched fig pudding to Dennis's distress.

"As a matter of fact, we're getting along pretty well considering we've only put in a couple of hours so far," he remarked. "I didn't realize before how badly I needed an assistant."

"Assistant! Ha!" Margo turned to where Emma was fighting the flood of color that threatened to engulf her for no reason at all. "So you've been promoted, Tamplin? Well, take it from somebody who knows more about Dan Slater than the law allows—don't go falling for the big ape! He's married to that dry rag of his and when it comes to the entertainment section, well, he's got all the help he needs—help that would put you in the . . ."

"I think we can adjourn to the living room now," Dan said quietly, a light in his narrowed eyes that made Emma decide she had things to do in her own room.

"Just a minute, Tamplin," Margo said softly as Dan led his nephew from the room, chatting about tomorrow's plans and the likelihood of locating a good shoal for clams.

It irritated Emma intensely, that habit Margo had of calling her by her last name, as if she were a piece of office furniture instead of a person. She waited, looking over her shoulder impatiently. She might owe her being here to

Margo Summerlin, but it was Dan Slater who employed her now, and she didn't have to put up with any more of Margo's condescension.

"My own crew will be coming down here in a few days for the Halpern interview and there'll be more than enough clerical help for Dan, so if you've something pressing back home—the boyfriend, for instance—then don't let us keep you. We could use your room, as a matter of fact."

"If Mr. Slater wants me to go, Miss Summerlin, he'll tell me. I'm working for him now, not you," Emma declared, struggling to maintain a cool control over her explosive temper.

Light brown eyes narrowed, taking on a look of tarnished brass. "For your own good, Tamplin, I'm going to tell you something. Dan Slater is too kind when it comes to picking up waifs and strays—look at the way he got himself saddled with the kid for the whole damned summer! But when it comes to moonstruck little typists who practically throw themselves across his bed, he soon gets a bellyful! And you're just the latest in a line a mile long, I can assure you! Not that it matters that much to me, because when I'm ready to settle down, I'll marry him, and that will put an end to his leisure-time hobbies." She smiled, and it wasn't a pleasant thing to see. "Oh, yes. Don't pop those jelly-bean eyes out at me. I've been asked, all right, and whenever I snap my fingers Dan will come a-running—don't ever doubt it."

From a coldness that pierced her clean through, Emma managed to dredge up a calm answer. "Mr. Slater's personal plans are nothing to do with me, Miss Summerlin."

"Exactly. Dan always bends over backward to be democratic to the hired help, Tamplin, but just a friendly warning for your own sake—don't read anything in it that's not there."

Hiding her anguished feelings behind a tilted chin and a straight back, Emma stepped inside her room and softly closed the door. The sweeping beam of the lighthouse that usually brought her so much delight was ignored as she sank down stiffly onto her bed.

Well, she had wondered—now she knew. They were engaged to be married, and if Margo didn't wear a ring to warn off other would-be contenders, it was probably because she wasn't the type for jewelry. What was it Dan had said about that kiss he had claimed today? It wasn't that type?

Maybe for him it wasn't, but for Emma it was a warning, in case she hadn't already got the message, that for the sake of her own mental health, she'd better be getting out of here as fast as she could. Too basically honest a person to hide her feelings very successfully, she was bound to reveal the foolish infatuation she had developed. To be laughed at by both Dan and Margo would utterly destroy her!

Chapter Five

It was too hot to sleep. The ceiling fan had been struggling against overwhelming odds, making the air merely bearable when she had finally fallen into a troubled sleep. She had awakened several times, though—always with a feeling of unease she couldn't explain. She agreed in principle with Dan's attitude toward artificially created atmosphere and the long-term effects of growing used to overcooling and overheating, but just this once she could have appreciated a small air conditioner.

She awakened again to an uncanny stillness—not a breath of air, nor a glimmer of light anywhere—and she had been dreaming of Derek. In her dreams an enormous wave had been following her, threatening to engulf her, and through some strange transmogriphication the wave became Derek, and she was swimming as fast as she could to the shelter of Dan's outstretched arms.

For several unreal minutes Emma sat there in the darkness, her heart pounding with a frantic, shallow rhythm, and then it dawned on her that her fan had stopped. She reached out to the bedside lamp and clicked the switch impotently, then climbed out of bed, the hot air striking her damp body in the short nylon gown with an unpleasant clamminess. The light switch beside the door didn't work either. The power must have gone off.

Standing hesitantly in the hallway, wondering whether or not she should awaken anyone, she caught an odd glimmer through a window in the living room. She felt her way through the suffocating darkness to stare out at a flame that seemed to begin and end in the sky.

Thoroughly frightened now, with that mindless terror that rises so easily between midnight and dawn, she turned to make her way back across the unfamiliar room and stumbled over a toy Dennis had left on the floor. It hadn't hurt, nor had she done more than catch herself on a table, but the sound—a gasp and the rattle of a cup and saucer—was enough to arouse someone. She heard a door open and close further down the hall.

"Who is it?" she whispered.

"Emma?"

Dan's voice was soft, yet not quite a whisper. He came unerringly to where she stood, uncertain of where to go or what to do.

"Dan," she whispered tensely, "there's a fire and the power's off."

"Where?" he demanded quickly.

"Out there." She pointed, forgetting that he couldn't see her in the thick darkness. "Out the window." Even as she spoke there came the sound of a fire engine and signs of activity in the vicinity of the eerie blaze and Dan caught her shoulders, moved her to one side, and strode with sure steps to the window. "It's a pole fire," he told her after a moment. "That accounts for the loss of power."

Edging closer to where he stood faintly silhouetted against the dark glow of the sky, she asked what a pole fire was.

"Salt collects on the insulators and shorts them out. Hot wires catch the poles and you have a pole fire. Happens a lot down here," he told her calmly. "One of the hazards of island atmosphere. They seem to have it under control now, but there's no telling when the power will come on again."

"I don't care about the lights, but I can't seem to breathe without the fan," she allowed, drawing closer to the comfort of that broad back.

"Try the porch. There might be a breath of air stirring out there. Come on, we'll see." He caught her wrist and led her to the door and she followed him blindly, even while her mind was screaming at her not to be such a fool.

"Ah, this is better. Here, the cushions are damp and it'll feel good. Move over."

Not again, she cried silently. "Dan, I think I'd better go to my room," she blurted, resisting when he would have urged her down onto the cushioned lounger.

"Why? You've just admitted you can't breathe inside."

She was having even more trouble catching her breath out here, although she didn't dare tell him so.

"What are you afraid of, Emma?" he asked softly as his hands closed over her shoulders and shook her ever so gently.

"I'm not afraid of anything," she lied valiantly.

"If you're not afraid of the dark, then it must be this you're afraid of." He drew her close to him and she hadn't the strength to resist. It was as if she had known from the moment she had awakened from that disturbing dream that this was going to happen. She only wanted to let go the inhibitions of a lifetime, to throw away common sense and let nature take its course. On a night like this—hot, still, and dark, laden with delicious, seductive scents from exotic shrubs just outside—common sense had no place.

His mouth found hers and with an impatient, muffled word he drew her hard against his body, making her aware for the first time that he wore only a pair of pajama pants, riding low on lean hips. Heat sprang to life between them. He forced her arms up over his shoulders, hunching over to reach down to her upturned face, and then he lifted her, dragging her up over the hard contours of his body until she could only cling to him helplessly, allowing him to plunder her lips with a kiss that made her senses reel.

She hung suspended by his hurting strength, her thin gown rucked up between them and then

he lay her on the lounge, following her heavily
with his own weight. His mouth found the hollow under her ear and traced the course of the
tendon, setting off brushfires along the way, and
his hands did away with the fragile barrier
between them. A boneless lethargy overtook
her. She felt his hard grip on the curve of her
waist, the stunning touch of his hand as it
splayed over her abdomen and then his teeth
caught the dusky, hard nub of her breast with
exquisite control, driving her into little incoher-
ent murmurings.

A terrible, tender pressure grew inside her
until it threatened to swallow her up, and it was
only the feel of his hands as they slid the elastic
of her pants lower that brought her to her shuddering senses again. She stiffened and protested—only a whisper at first, but he heard her.
"No, Dan . . . please . . . no."

"Yes, Emma, please . . . yes," he groaned in
the sweet valley between her throbbing breasts.

She caught at his hands, stilling them in their
devastating exploration, and he allowed her that
much, but he didn't lift his weight from her, nor
stop the liquifying caresses of his tongue.

Her stiffness gradually got through to him and
he lifted his head to stare down at her in the
darkness. "Why, Emma?" He was very still.

The question echoed in her mind, bringing
back to her the one she had asked him earlier
about his first kiss. Why had he kissed her then?
Why did he want to make love to her now? Was it
as Margo had hinted—that until he allowed
himself to marry he considered himself a free
agent and any gullible female a likely target?

"You mean why not, don't you?" She tried for lightness and failed miserably and he sat up, turned his back to her, and lighted a cigarette. In the brief flare of the match she saw the outline of his tumbled hair, the shape of his hands, still a trifle unsteady, and she smelled the scent of tobacco as it mingled with the fragrance of oleanders and the piny, musky scent of his body.

"All right then, why not?" He sounded tense and impatient and she winced, illogically wanting to draw him back to her arms.

"Because I don't . . . I mean, I'm not used to . . ."

"To sleeping around?" he finished crudely.

"Yes." The word was tiny, brittle, and it seemed to hover in the air between them until he shattered it with a hard, short laugh.

"The lady's prerogative. It's a little hard to believe in this day and age, and you were willing enough."

That hurt. The pain shafted deep and twisted inside her but she only lifted her chin and waited until it faded. "What about Margo?"

He turned at that, casting her a look over his shoulder before speaking. "What has Margo got to do with it?"

The lump in her throat almost prevented her from speaking but she continued doggedly. "She . . . you're . . . well, you did ask her to marry you." The pause stretched unbearably. "Didn't you?" she whispered miserably.

She thought he wasn't going to answer and in a quick burgeoning of anger she wriggled herself to the foot of the lounge and stood up, her hands on her hips, to glare at him in the glowing darkness.

"Well?" she persisted masochistically.

"Yes. I did."

"Then how dare you . . ." She took a deep breath and started over again. "How dare you try to make love to me when you're . . . when you . . ."

"All right, Emma," he sighed tiredly. "You can cut the outraged virgin act. You're perfectly safe from me from now on, so don't worry."

"You're darned right I'm safe from you, Dan Slater! If I didn't need this job I'd get out of here tonight and let you do your own stupid typing!"

"Of course you won't leave. It's not all that easy to get good office help down here and you've proven an asset in just one morning, so don't go blowing one kiss into a major melodrama. If I don't turn you on, then I don't turn you on. Believe me, I won't be wasting away from unrequited love."

Emma caught her breath and then let it out in a shaky stream. "*Mr.* Slater, allow me to inform you that you're a first-rate jerk and that I'll work for you because I need the money, but at the end of three weeks you can just find yourself someone else. And if it makes you feel any safer, I won't be breaking my heart over you, either!"

"So there, too," he said grinning, applauding slowly, insolently, three times as she turned and stalked out just as if she could see where she was going. She made it as far as the toy on the floor and she went down painfully, cursing Dennis's untidy habits.

Dan was beside her in an instant, his hands

easing her up and holding her against escape. "Are you all right?" he demanded gruffly. The concern in his voice was unmistakable, as was the gentle touch of his hands as they grazed her shoulders, her arms, and then went up to brush the hair from her face.

"Yes, thank you," she answered stiffly.

"Emma . . . I'm sorry. I was way out of line and the only excuse I can offer is extreme provocation. Let's go back and start over, can we? Please?"

She was helpless against the power of his deep, resonant voice. For the last time she tried for reason and logic and all the important guidelines for a sane, trouble-free life. Then she kissed them good-bye, recognizing the naked truth. As illogical as it was, she was in love with this man and she'd stay as long as he would have her under whatever conditions he laid out and deal with the heartbreak when it came the best way she could.

"Friends?" he asked now.

"Friends," she agreed fatalistically.

The weatherman called it an inversion, Mrs. Pugh said it was all those smokestacks they have up north, but all Emma knew was that it was thick and still and terribly depressing outside. The promise of rain remained unfulfilled, but at least the power was on again.

In spite of the fact that they planned to catch and cook a variety of seafood, Mrs. Pugh sent them off with a heavy hamper and Dan added a large cooler of drinks to the load in the back of the jeep. Dennis was bounding about on the hard bench already, regaling them with his prowess as a hunter of clams. Margo, from the front seat, sent him a disparaging look that made Emma draw the wriggling boy closer to her side protectively. Not that Dennis needed her protection. He squirmed out from under her arm and checked the dip nets to see that they were not in need of mending and began telling them both the best way to catch hard crabs.

Mary was waiting at her house for them, calling out that Field had already gone to gas up. She closed her door and came along with them in the jeep, holding her plastic beach bag on her lap. "Got something for sun, Emma? You've got a nice tan for a redhead, but there aren't all that many trees out where we're goin'."

"I didn't think about a hat," Emma confessed, "but I did bring along a long-sleeved shirt in case it got cool."

"Dream on!"

They pulled up at the delapidated wharf within minutes and Dennis was over the tailgate, his skinny little legs going like pistons. Field was doing something on board a beautiful boat—not the sleek fiberglass yacht Emma had expected, but one of the older wooden fishing boats with its high, graceful bow and low, rounded stern.

Margo halted halfway down the footpath and demanded to know what had happened to the *Moonglow*.

"Oh, did I forget to mention she was in Wanchese today? Sorry, Margo, ol' gal," Field said with what Emma could have sworn was a tongue-in-cheek grin at Dan.

Mary, settling the hampers of food in the

small open cabin, said that Field wasn't satisfied until he had every gadget known to man and the new boat was being fixed up with a fish finder—her derisive tone indicating her opinion of the electronic device.

"I noticed the name is the *L. Mary*," Emma said. "What's the L. for?"

Field and Mary simply grinned at each other and for the rest of the day sporadic attempts were made to fathom the secret the married couple seemed to derive so much pleasure from. They tried *Lucky Mary, Lady Mary, Lovely Mary*, and any number of farfetched combinations, but to Emma's frustrated amusement, the secret remained intact.

Margo had brought along an elegant briefcase and when Field provided her with a folding lounge chair, she stretched out, cool and lovely in white sharkskin slacks and halter, in the shade of the canvas canopy and proceeded to dig into reams of reading matter. Dan picked up one of her sheafs of what looked to be photocopies of clippings and he lanced her with a swift, tight-lipped look, but no words passed between them. When Field dropped anchor over a shoal and ordered abandon ship, Dan and Dennis, their browned bodies clad only in the briefest of white trunks, dove off the cabin together, slicing neatly through the glassy aquamarine waters of the Pamlico.

There was a breeze. Not enough to break the surface of the water into more than finger waves, and often even that faded away, but it was cool enough, even under the relentless sun that beat down from a cloudless sky. Emma was soon scrambling up on the top of the cabin to dive in along with the others. Field, wearing a pair of baggy shorts that sagged under a slight paunch, nevertheless looked surprisingly fit, his grizzled hair contrasting with his mahogany skin. To Emma's amusement, he and Mary cavorted with Dennis and Dan and herself as lightheartedly as if they were half their own age. Field confessed that he was the only one of his brothers who could swim. Mary had refused to marry him until he had learned.

"*Learning Mary*? No, that doesn't make sense," Emma exclaimed.

"Try *Leering Mary,* or maybe *Lustful Mary,*" Field suggested.

"Darn you, Fielding, you quit that!" Mary cried out, splashing her husband and getting herself ducked as a result.

Ferrying the gear ashore to a small island that seemed to float greenly in space on the mirror-like water, Dan soon organized the various individuals into clammers, crabbers, and fishermen, while Margo continued to read on board. Emma hopped awkwardly through the shallows with Dennis while he scooped up plate-sized crabs, and then she was called on to wade out with more bait to where Field and Mary were fishing in the channel.

When Mary called over her shoulder to remind Emma not to get too burned, Margo volunteered her own sunscreen. Emma, masking her surprise, slathered the scented liquid over her face, arms, and shoulders.

"Don't forget your legs," Margo reminded her.

"I hate to use so much," Emma protested,

standing hip deep in the water several yards
away from where the boat was at anchor.

"Help yourself. You see my tan—that's the
only brand I ever use, and I buy it by the gallon,
so feel free."

Emma did. The combination of sun and salt
water made her skin feel dry and tingly, but at
least she had some protection. Once she showered off tonight, she'd have a delectable tan to
take back to Washington with her.

Pushing away the thought of returning to the
stifling apartment and the monotonous rounds
of offices, she set herself out to enjoy the day.
She floundered eagerly along beside Dan as he
dove for clams in deeper water, carried Mary's
catch ashore for her, and learned how to clean
the crabs from Dennis.

They cooked on the island and Margo deigned
to put down her reading matter long enough to
join them. She emerged from the cabin in a
sleek white bikini, revealing a flawless figure.
She made Emma, in her faded one-piece suit,
feel dowdier than ever—especially as she was
also wearing Dan's handkerchief knotted on all
four corners as a hat.

Field had cooked clams, crabs, and fish together in a big tub of salt water scooped up from
the Sound. He had poured in a bottle of vinegar
and almost a bottleful of hot sauce and Emma
had been more than a little doubtful of the
outcome. After the first cautious taste, she had
fallen to with the rest of them. When she fished
out a piece of crab and looked at it skeptically, it
was Dan who moved in behind her and, reaching over her shoulders, showed her how to break

it apart to reveal the succulent morsels of white meat. With the juice dripping down her arms, Emma laughed up over her shoulder at him, her stomach tightening at the feel of his nearness. Then she caught sight of Margo, her face shuttered behind dark glasses, but her lips thinned in that now familiar line, and a small rush of disquiet overcame her.

It was gone in a minute. Margo had been far more friendly today than at any time since Emma had been here on the Banks, and while the men cleaned up the remains of the feast, Margo dispelled Emma's momentary doubts by offering to anoint her back for her.

The touch of the cold liquid both hurt and soothed and Emma sucked in her breath, bowing her head to allow Margo to do her neck and shoulders.

"Does it hurt?" the older woman asked solicitously, capping the bottle and dropping it into her capacious bag.

"Not too much. I expect I'm chaffed from the straps of my suit as much as anything. I've worn it all day long. Thanks, Margo." She strolled over to where the men stood skipping clamshells out into the Sound. "Littering?" she asked impudently.

"Layin' a foundation for next year's oysters," Field retorted, handing her a wet shell to dispose of. She chunked it and it disappeared heavily beneath the surface, bringing on a spate of criticisms of her style. Once again it was Dan who stood behind her to show her the proper way to get the maximum number of skips from any shell.

When his hands rested on her shoulder, she winced away and he tipped a questioning glance down at her face. "Too much sun?"

"Too much everything," she admitted ruefully, "but I wouldn't have missed a minute of it!"

By the time they started back the sun was a sullen red orb half hidden by slate gray clouds. A fresh breeze had sprung up and Emma was glad of the long-sleeved shirt and only wished she had brought along a pair of slacks as well. Mary asked if her skin was sore, but Emma laughed off the rapidly increasing discomfort. "No more than I deserve, and a small price to pay for all the fun I've had today. Honestly, Mary, I've never had such a good time in my life! I don't know how I'm going to stand being back in the city again."

The engines throbbed monotonously and Emma's eyelids began to droop. She waited until Dan closed the starboard cockpit locker with its bench top and then she crossed the small space and stretched out on it, wincing as her tender flesh came into contact with the hard painted surface.

Back at the wharf in the creek that ran behind Field's home, Emma found she could barely move. Under the cover of her shirt, she slipped down the straps of her bathing suit, alleviating some of the acute discomfort, but it was almost more than she could do to hide her misery while the leavetakings were made. Dennis secured permission to stay with Field and Mary for a few days, so he could go on a fishing and camping trip with the Adams—close neighbors of the Slaters who had two boys his age; so there was only the three of them returning to Larkin's Ridge.

While Dan stayed behind for a last word with his cousin, Margo waited in the front seat of the jeep, watching with sardonic amusement as Emma made her labored way into the back. Before either of them could speak, however, Dan appeared and levered himself under the wheel, sparing neither of his passengers a glance. From the little Emma could see from where she huddled over, trying to ease the fire in her back, a word from Dan at the moment wouldn't be very pleasant. For some reason she was too tired to try and unravel, he had lost all of his earlier good humor. Maybe he had quarreled with Field. No, that was ridiculous. They had clapped each other on the shoulder as they parted. Whatever was wrong, it had nothing to do with Field or his wife.

With Emma, herself, then? Surely not with Margo.

Oh, give it up, Emma, it's nothing to do with you—hopefully. She was far too wrapped up in her own troubles to spare much thought for the couple in the front seat. Tremors were beginning to take hold of her and her stomach wasn't any too easy, either. Not only that, she was freezing cold. All in the world she wanted to do now was to crawl off somewhere and burrow down in a pile of blankets and lose herself in sleep before the situation worsened.

Pulling the jeep up in front of the house, Dan jumped out and turned to where Emma sat, braced against the roughness of the ride. "Here, let me give you a hand," he said with surprising kindness, considering the slightly grim look that still lingered around his mouth and his eyes.

"I can manage," she gritted, extending a leg cautiously. She climbed out awkwardly, declining his hand, and when she straightened up, her knees almost buckled under her. Hard pain slammed into the tender, burned flesh at the backs of her legs as the circulation resumed, and as if that weren't enough, she still felt as if she were on board the *L. Mary*.

She made it slowly up the three steps, flinching away when Dan would have offered her assistance, and she was dimly aware that while he held the door open for her to precede him, he caught Margo's arm and kept her outside. Beyond caring about anything except finding relief from the exquisite torture assailing her body, Emma left them and sought the sanctuary of her own room. She had heard of people being allergic to sunscreen, but . . .

But was it sunscreen? "Oh, no, she wouldn't," she groaned to the empty room.

Half an hour later, Emma had managed to shower herself off, removing at least the irritation of the salt that had dried on her skin. The cool water had felt so good she was reluctant to leave it. At last she surrendered to inevitability and stepped out, flinging out her arms to catch herself when her head began to reel. She patted herself dry and located a soft white nylon gown made along the lines of a choir robe. It touched her shoulders lightly and skimmed to the floor, and feeling as if she were still on board the rolling deck, she made her way slowly across the bedroom and collapsed on her bed.

She could have been asleep for hours, or only minutes; she dimly recalled hearing angry voices and the slamming of a car door, but since her lights were still on she lost all sense of time. She decided drowsily that if it were breakfast time, she wasn't interested.

Someone rapped softly on her door and reluctantly she opened her eyes again. Before she could respond, the door opened and Dan let himself in. He had changed into something dark and close fitting and he quickly crossed to stand looking down at her, lines of concern on his shadowed face as he reached out a hand to touch her blazing forehead.

"Doesn't look so good, little one," he murmured tightly, concern edging his voice as he slipped aside the neck of her gown and frowned at what he saw.

Her mouth opened to tell him what had happened, but then she refrained. What was the use? If he didn't know already what a horror he was planning to marry then he wouldn't appreciate anyone's enlightening him at this late date. She merely groaned when he touched her lightly on the throat under her chin.

"Even here—from the reflections, I guess. Honey, you've got to put something on to ease that burn. I think there's an aloe vera lotion in the cabinet. I'll go get it while you get yourself out of that Mother Hubbard you're wearing. Be right back."

A few moments later he returned to find Emma as he had left her—on her back with the sheet and spread pulled up to her chin. She was trembling uncontrollably now, feeling the hard, racking chills coursing through her slight body. Above the white covers, her eyes pleaded with him with far more eloquence than she could know.

Gently, he removed the covers from her clutching fingers and folded them back to the foot of the bed. He lifted her gown to bare her legs and in a reassuringly matter-of-fact way began smoothing on the comforting lotion. At first it seemed cold, but then the coldness was replaced with a heavenly warmth that stole the fire from her skin. When he ordered her to turn over, she obeyed wordlessly.

The magic of his hands touched her, stroking the balm on her legs and then, pushing her gown up, on her back and her poor, tortured shoulders, taking the pain away with such effectiveness that Emma allowed herself to forget the fact that her gown was laid neatly back over her head. There could be nothing erotic about a body in the condition hers was in and she was too far gone in drowsy contentment to protest when he lifted her ever so carefully and turned her onto her back again, pulling back down her nightgown.

"Is that a functional drawstring or just a pretty bow?" he asked quizzically.

Her hands went to the white satin ribbon at her neck. "It's a drawstring," she admitted weakly, her eyes never leaving the dark strength of his face.

"Draw it."

She pulled the end of the bow and eased the filmy gown down over the tops of her shoulders and then Dan placed the bottle on the bedside table and lifted her to a sitting position while he lowered the gown. He eased her arms through the flowing sleeves and she stared helplessly up into his shuttered face while he spread the rest of the lotion over her shoulders, arms, her throat, and then he allowed his fingers to caress her face with the soothing coolness before stepping back abruptly.

"Get some rest now." He bit off the words curtly, with none of the gentleness his touch had revealed. "I'll bed down in Dennis's room with both doors open in between in case you need me in the night."

She protested but he silenced her effectively. "Would you rather have Margo?"

Once, just before daylight, she roused from a nightmare, moaning in a state of limbo between the terror of her dream and the misery of awakening.

Dan was beside her almost instantly. "It's all right now, little one, I'm here," he murmured, touching her hair with an infinitely gentle hand. Once more he applied the lotion, turning her to lower her gown as if he were a patient nurse, and Emma was helpless in the hands of such kindness. Her skin was on fire and she was thirsty and she thought her heart would burst with love for the man who bared her body with the impersonal concern he might have offered his nephew in similar circumstances. Not by a flicker of an eyelid did he reveal that he was moved by the intimate vision of her body.

Afterward, he brought her a glass of cool water and waited while she finished it, lowering her and bringing up the spread again. The racking chills had gone and now she only felt bruised all over. She closed her eyes, afraid to look at him, afraid of what he might read in her face in the gray light of morning.

Mrs. Pugh served her breakfast in bed, tsk-tsking at her burns. She came later to help her dress when Emma insisted on getting up for lunch and Emma asked curiously where everyone was. The house had been unnaturally quiet all morning, except when Mary had phoned to see how she was.

"Mr. Dan's gone out somewheres and the boy's gone off on that fishin' trip with the Adams. I believe Miss Summerlin left last night. Leastwise, she wasn't here when I got here and her things is missin'."

Bursting with curiosity, Emma hobbled over and sat gingerly on a chair, wondering now if Dan had, in fact, been aware of Margo's behavior on the picnic, and if that had been the subject of their argument last night. Her heart swelled with hope. "Will Dan be back for lunch . . . did he say?"

"Lord, no tellin'. Them Slaters is a come-an'-go bunch if ever there was one. I known 'em all, since they was divin' nekkid off the dock, knee high to a sea turtle. If he comes, he comes, if he don't, we wait."

Chapter Six

Three days elapsed before Emma was allowed to begin work again. Dan was impersonally friendly and she wondered if he regretted sending Margo away. She found herself aching for a return to their former interludes of closeness. Whether he was ministering to her ailments or making love to her, anything was preferable to this cool, polite office relationship.

Her typing speed suffered and her concentration wasn't what it should have been because she was far too conscious of the restless dark figure who paced the length of the cool, book-lined room.

Reginald Fessenden. She forced her mind back to what Dan was saying about the man who had developed an entirely new system of wireless transmission. It was based on a different principle from that of Lodge, Marconi, and all the others, and it eventually proved to be the correct one. Marconi got the credit that was due Fessenden, but it was Fessenden who first effected two-way trans-Atlantic service, between Massachussetts and Scotland in 1906. He invented the wireless telephone, made the first radio broadcast in history, invented the Fathometer, the submarine telephone, turboelectric drives for battleships, and he pioneered short-wave radio. Much of his earliest work was done right on Hatteras Island. He was sending messages between Buxton and Manteo as early as 1901 and 1902.

"If he was such an important inventor, why haven't I ever heard of him before?" Emma had asked during one of their first sessions.

"He was a genius, all right, only not much of a businessman. His patents were seized, his ideas stolen, and one of the world's biggest corporations acquired rights to his major discoveries, but poor Reginald never got a cent from it."

Now, in the stillness of late summer, Emma found herself staring at Dan's well-developed shoulders, at the lithe line of his powerful thighs revealed by the worn jeans he worked in. She recalled the first time she had ever seen him, bending over buckets of fish, those same jeans riding low on his hips as the sun glinted off the sweat on his back.

"Did you get that last?" he demanded impatiently.

"What last?" She came out of her daydream to see him glaring down at her.

"Come down out of the clouds! Are you still waiting for that boyfriend to show up?"

For a moment Emma puzzled over his words and then she remembered Derek's call. Good Heavens! She had forgotten all about it! The boyfriend, she thought ironically—if he only knew!

And then, in one of those coincidences that are stranger than fiction, the phone rang. Dan picked it up to bark into the receiver and then handed it to her.

Hesitantly, she took the receiver from him and spoke. "Hello?" And then: "Hugh! Where are you?"

It turned out that her stepbrother was on the island, booked in at a motel near the lighthouse in Buxton. They made arrangements to get together in his room at eight. Since he'd just got in, he told her he was going to sleep until his stomach woke him up for dinner.

When Emma put down the phone, it was to find that Dan had left the room. She followed him out only to see him slam the door of his car and leave with a speed that left dust hovering in the air for several minutes. Her shoulders lifted in an expression of disdain. If that was all his work meant to him, then she'd take a break herself, even though it was only ten twenty in the morning.

Dan hadn't arrived by the time Mrs. Pugh put the cold supper on and left for the day. After she had gone, Emma sat at the table, her mind going back relentlessly to Dan and his strange, changeable moods.

She had thought at first that he was upset over her taking a personal call during work hours, but then she told herself that that was ridiculous. Moody he might be on occasion, but Dan would never be petty. And besides, he had been odd ever since Margo had left, the night of the boat trip.

Perhaps he was missing her. There didn't seem to be much romance between the pair of them—at least not while Emma was at hand—but then maybe people of their sophisticated background played it cool. For all her twenty-four years and her big-city background, Emma was relatively inexperienced in affairs of the heart. Hugh had once teased her about being a late-blooming snapdragon, but she knew it hadn't been only that.

She had always been romantic where men were concerned, and it came as a gradual let-down to her that few, if any, of the men who asked her out measured up to the private yard-stick she carried in her heart. Until Dan Slater. He measured up to the extent that she threw away her ruler; from now on, the men in her life, if there ever were any, would be held up against Dan's singular qualifications. She knew without having to dwell on it that none would measure up. Nowhere would she ever find that magic combination of character, intelligence, tenderness, and humor that could set her mind adrift on uncharted seas at the same time he set her body aflame with unfulfilled desires.

She loved him. It was as simple as that, and for all their few brief moments, someone else had a prior claim.

She put away the food and rinsed the dishes before dressing carefully for her meeting with Hugh. Somewhere in the depths of her mind was a disquieting question of why he had come here. What about his job? What about his debts?

Carefully making her way to her car in her high-heeled sandals, she closed her mind to speculation. She'd know soon enough why he found it necessary to follow her down here.

The sweeping beam of the lighthouse guided her south on highway 12. The days were getting shorter now; only a few weeks ago, it would still have been light and now the sky was a bruised rose color, fast fading into midnight blue behind her. Thinking of her stepbrother inevitably carried her thoughts back to Washington and she acknowledged with a hollow feeling that all too soon she'd be headed back there. She could pay off Derek once and for all—if she didn't eat for a month or so. After a while the whole Hatteras episode would begin to fade around the edges. She knew all too well, though, that there would be painful times when her mind would look back and imagine Dan, dressed in the familiar jeans, his hands dexterously working with a net or clumsily typing his manuscript. She experienced a presentiment of the pain that would be hers when she no longer shared the house at Larkin's Ridge with him.

Locating the room with no trouble, Emma rapped lightly, hoping Hugh had awakened from his nap.

"Come in," she was invited over the drone of the air conditioner. She pushed the door ajar and looked into the dimly lighted room. Hugh was bent over the foot of the bed, tying his shoes, and she smiled as she crossed the carpet, only when he turned to greet her it was not Hugh at all but Derek Villers.

Emma clutched her midsection and took a backward step, as if she could go out and enter again and it would all come right, but it wouldn't. Her brother wasn't in evidence, and instead, Derek, his nondescript brown hair brushed back over his too pale face, greeted her with a practiced smile.

"Where's Hugh?" she demanded, ignoring the outstretched hand.

"Still dining, I suppose. I suggested he might like to take the car and look around for any signs of life in the place. Come in, Emma, and let me look at you." The smile that revealed perfect teeth remained pasted in place, but the small eyes were watchful. "Come on, now, don't be shy. Old Derek missed you, baby—didn't you know that?"

"I came to see my brother, Mr. Villers. You can tell him for me that if he has time before he goes back to see me to call and we'll make arrangements."

"Now, don't be that way, Little Emma. Call me Derek, I'm your friend, you know that." He was close enough now so that Emma could see the gleam of oily perspiration on his high forehead and it made her shudder. It was so totally different from the clean, honest sweat of Dan's well-conditioned body. She was reminded forcefully of the dim, smoky club where she had gone just once to see Hugh after he had started moonlighting there.

"Good-bye, Mr. Villers," she said firmly, backing out the door.

He moved more swiftly than she would have thought he could, catching her by the wrist and dragging her back inside. He eased the pressure, stroking her hand with his own hot, damp palm. "Not so fast, girl. You might as well know that your brother and I have come to an . . . a sort of understanding. Since it concerns you, you might as well know about it."

"I'm not interested in any understanding you have with Hugh, Mr. Villers," she said through stiff, cold lips. "As soon as we pay you off, neither of us will ever see you again, and you can bank on that!"

"Oh, pretty hoity-toity, aren't we? Did your precious brother tell you that he got involved in another game the other night and found lady luck deserting him, as usual?"

Nausea threatened to overcome her.

"No comment? Then maybe you'll have something to say to this. I've agreed to cancel all Hugh's debts on the day you marry me. Now, what do you think of that? Old Derek isn't such a bad fellow after all, is he? I mean, it's all in the family, so to speak."

It wasn't happening. Not another debt and certainly not Derek's insane proposal! Panic threatened to choke her as she pulled against his surprising strength. "I . . . I can't marry you, Mr. Villers," she pleaded.

"Then Hugh's employer hears the extent of his junior accountant's . . . uh . . . indiscretions. These things have a way of getting around, you know. He'll be lucky to get taken on as a bag boy for a small-town supermarket when word gets around."

Her frantic mind threw out the first defense she could think of. "I'm already married, Mr. Villers!"

His smile, even in the dim light of the single lamp, wasn't a nice thing to see and he chided her smoothly as his eyes went to her bare left hand. "Come on, Emma, you can't play games with old Derek and win. I eat little girls like you for breakfast."

"It's true! My rings . . . I left them off until I told Hugh."

He caught her wrist again and pulled her close enough so that she could smell the over-powering scent of his cologne. "Don't try to play me up, Emma Tamplin. I could have made you my mistress just as easily, and if you want to get cute, we'll do it that way. On second thought, I'm too smart to go taking on a stupid brother-in-law who can't get himself out of trouble without bellyaching to sis. What say we settle for some-thing a little more informal, hmmm?"

Seeing the large, shiny face looming closer, Emma leaned away from him, struggling to release her wrist. "It's . . . it's true, Mr. Villers . . . Derek! His name is Dan. I . . . I work for him and we fell in love and . . . and we were married last week!" Pure terror made her sound convincing for she was pleading for more than her life. If Derek Villers touched her she knew she'd die.

"Dan, is it?" Derek growled, his fingers biting into her flesh.

"Yes! The man I work for! Now, please let me go, or Dan will . . . he'll . . ."

She never got to finish. Hugh's voice called

from behind her. "Emma! There you are!" He came up behind her and threw an arm across her shoulders, hugging her to him as Derek released her wrist. "I went up to Avon to find you, but the Heathcliff type said you'd already gone. Don't tell me he's the one you're working for. I thought it was a woman, the one who does the special interest programs."

Derek answered for her, his voice rough and vaguely threatening. "Not only works for, Hughboy. You'd better start polishing up to your new brother-in-law because it looks like he's about all that stands between you and a new striped suit."

The explanations were made haltingly with Emma growing sicker every minute and Hugh casting nervous glances at the tall man who lounged against a dresser, his ankles crossed to reveal white silk socks above his shiny white loafers.

It was decided that Hugh would come to Larkin's Ridge at ten the next morning—alone. Emma insisted on that, and then she made her escape, wondering if she should begin her one-way swim to Diamond Shoals now or wait until tomorrow.

On the way back to the Ridge her mind flailed her with accusations. How could she have been so stupid? She could have invented someone—she might even have stalled until she finished the job and could pay Derek off, but then there was that additional debt. Oh, Lord, how could he have managed to mire himself even deeper?

With a feeling of dread sureness, she knew that no matter what Hugh did, Derek would have managed to draw him in until he was way over his head. Hugh was Derek's means of getting to Emma and for some unfathomable reason, he had decided to have her. Why, she couldn't imagine, for there were countless girls with far more claim to beauty. She had heard that middle-aged men sometimes tried to recapture their youth with innocent, young girls, but she wasn't all that young, and how could Derek know about her past inexperience? She didn't exactly advertise it and surely she was as worldly and sophisticated as her peers in all but that one respect.

Parking automatically in her usual place, she sat there in the dark, her hands clutching the steering wheel as she sought a way out of the mess she had landed herself in. As she saw it, she had three choices: she could confess her lie to Hugh and beg his help and could even go so far as to tell Derek frankly that she had lied and then borrow the money from somewhere to pay him off immediately. Or she could tell Dan what she had done and ask him to pretend, just for now, to be her husband. If she could only hold off until she finished the rest of her time here she could pay off the largest part of the first debt. Hugh would simply have to take care of the second one himself. She had about concluded that it was no favor to her brother to continually be bailing him out of one fix after another.

Taking a deep, steadying breath, she let herself out of the car, still undecided on what course to take. Her high heels wobbled on the rough, uneven marl and she wondered irrelevantly if she might have been better able to cope

with Derek if she could have looked him square-
ly in the eye. At a fraction over five feet tall, she
had always been slightly intimidated by taller
people and she had all but exhausted her supply
of defensive weapons protecting herself against
Margo Summerlin.

A tiny red glow arced through the darkness of
the porch and Emma paused uncertainly.

"Emma?" Dan's quiet voice floated out on the
soft, fragrant air.

"Yes, it's me."

"You're home early, aren't you?" He sounded
strange, as if he were under some sort of tension,
and she answered carefully that she wasn't all
that early.

It was dark as pitch and he couldn't see her,
thank goodness, but something in her voice
must have alerted him. "Come here, Emma."

"I think I'll just go on inside now, Dan. I . . .
it's . . . I'm tired," she answered in a voice that
sounded unlike her own.

"Come here, Emma," Dan insisted calmly,
coming down the steps to meet her. He took her
arm and she allowed herself to be led back up on
the porch and into the screened portion. With
the decision taken from her unresisting hands,
she gave in, knowing she couldn't sleep, anyway, until she settled matters one way or another. It was far better to tackle him out here in the
kind darkness than inside under the all-too-
revealing light.

Even in that she was thwarted, however, for
Dan led her over to the lounge and then snapped
on the overhead light. Caught unawares, she
stared up at him, fear and embarrassment

struggling in her overbright eyes. His disconcertingly intent gaze missed nothing, touching on the tremor that assailed her bottom lip. Defiance thrust out her chin and she stared back at him, willing her fragile control not to break. She couldn't even speak to request that he turn out the light, but then he read her mind and switched it off, allowing her the shelter of enveloping darkness.

"What happened?"

"I don't know what you mean," she temporized.

The edges of his voice roughened. "Don't give me that! You left here all dolled up to go see the boyfriend. Meanwhile some wet-behind-the-ears punk roars up in a flashy car to see you. And to top it off, you're back within an hour looking as if you've been scared out of your wits! What is it, Emma—and don't tell me you don't know what I mean!"

She bit her lip to keep from pouring out the whole sordid, ridiculous mess, thankful for the darkness that hid her helpless tears.

"Emma? He didn't . . . he didn't hurt you, did he?"

The last thread of her brittle composure frayed and she choked on a sound that was somewhere between a laugh and a sob. When she felt the hard, comforting grip of his hands bite into her shoulders, she blurted out hopelessly, "Oh, Dan, I'm a terrible fool! I've done something so stupid, so . . . so unreasonable, I don't know how to tell you."

"Start from the beginning," he suggested with a calmness that was contagious.

In an agony of embarrassment she proceeded to tell him the bare essentials. If he had been only her employer instead of a man she loved so devastatingly, it wouldn't have been so bad. But when she came to the part about claiming him as her husband, her voice was a tiny thread that scarcely pierced the evening chorus of cicadas and tree frogs.

"I told you I was a fool," she said, gulping, her fingernails biting into the perspiring palms of her hands.

Dan lifted a fist and deliberately unfolded her fingers, stroking the wounded palms until she got her breathing under control again. "I won't argue that with you, Emma, but your foolishness was mainly in trying to shoulder your brother's mistakes. It doesn't help. Lessons of that sort can't be learned vicariously, unfortunately, and the damned cub was ready enough to throw you to the wolves."

What could she say? All along she had closed her mind to the fact that Hugh seemed perfectly willing to help Derek in his aims to promote some sort of a relationship with Emma. It was only this latest, the so-called agreement the two of them had cooked up, that opened her eyes to the lengths to which Hugh would go . . . or allow her to go, she amended bitterly.

"So what should I do now?" she asked Dan, sitting beside him in the darkness. She couldn't really see him, but she was acutely aware of the solid bulk of him beside her. It was intimidating, exciting, and infinitely comforting all at the same time. "Shall I tell them I lied or will you pretend to be . . . to be . . ."

"I don't think you'd get very far by confessing anything. You'd simply place yourself back in position number one," Dan mused slowly. Then, turning to her abruptly: "Will you trust me, Emma?"

"I do trust you, Dan, and I'm more sorry than I can say that I got you involved in all this ugly mess," she said helplessly.

"I'll see your stepbrother tomorrow, alone. As for you, you'll have to agree to go along with whatever I decide—is that clear?" His tone registered neither concern nor distaste now, only a very real determination tinged with what she could almost believe was excitement if it hadn't been so unreasonable.

She needed reassurance, she needed the comforting feel of his arms around her, and it was with a dragging reluctance that she stood up and bid him a hesitant good night.

"'Night, Emma. See you in the morning." He sounded utterly preoccupied and she was left with nothing to do but go to bed.

Chapter Seven

The next morning Emma bent over the small print of a long list of patents taken out in Reginald Fessenden's name and pretended to be absorbed in her work. Actually, she was far too conscious of her employer, who leaned back in the worn leather comfort of his dark green office chair as if completely engrossed in the copy of *Fessenden, Builder of Tomorrows* by the inventor's wife.

Wistfully, Emma studied him from the shield of her long lashes, taking in the beautiful shape of his well-developed forearms as they turned an occasional page. His jawline, that angular feature that showed the beginning of a shadow soon after lunch unless he shaved again, was relaxed, and his lips that could all too often rebuke with a chiseled firmness, now looked somehow different—sensual? Perhaps, but it was more as if a small, secret satisfaction curved their lines, as if his thoughts were of something more pleasurable than the unfortunate affairs of a man who had lived so long ago.

She forced her errant imagination to the task assigned her, and as her eyes followed the progress of her forefinger down the seemingly endless lists, she grew uncomfortably aware that this time she was the subject of study. Warm color crept up from beneath the low neckline of her yellow cotton shift and she allowed her hair to swing forward protectively against the burning scrutiny of Dan's eyes. Probably wondering how on earth he had got mixed up with her and her problems, she concluded.

Speculation was ended abruptly at the sound of tires on marl, and by the time the slamming of a car door announced the arrival of a visitor, Dan was on his feet, the book placed firmly on the top of his littered desk. "Stay here," he ordered, as if Emma had any idea of following him. He closed the door behind him, and she stared at the afterimage as his footsteps receded down the hallway. The tread was exactly like the man himself—firm, bold, confident—the sound of a man who knew exactly where he stood and where he was going.

Unlike some people I could mention, Emma thought with rueful self-deprecation. Somehow, with the best intentions in the world, she had managed to get herself involved in an affair that spelled ruin to any hopes of a happy-ever-after.

The rise and fall of masculine voices seemed to go on forever and Emma became aware that

her clutching fingers had creased the papers she
held beyond hope of repair. She was carefully,
nervously smoothing them out when Dan returned and closed the door to lean against it,
surveying her with a disconcertingly speculative
look.

She ducked her head and concentrated on
undoing the damage her carelessness had done.
His hand came out to lift her chin before she was
even aware that he had moved, and she stared
up at him apprehensively.

"Did he . . . did you tell him the truth?" she
faltered.

"Yes." He let it ride a moment, scanning her
face as if weighing something in his own mind.
"I told your stepbrother that we were to be
married as soon as the legalities could be taken
care of and that I'd settle with Villers on the
receipt of a written promise from him not to
involve you in any more of his affairs. No more
gambling, either, or he'd automatically cut all
ties with you."

Relief washed over her in huge floods, followed immediately by a reaction to what he had
said. "You told him . . . ? Oh. I guess that way
was better than the way I did it, after all. And
Dan, I promise to repay you every cent of what
you paid him. I'll work overtime—I'll be able to
double up when I get back to Washington, too,
and I thought about a list of the patents arranged according to category. It would make it
quicker for you to look something up, and then
I'll do you a list of those applied for and turned
down if it's possible."

He let her babble on, releasing some of the

enormous tension that had been growing in her since last night. Since long before that, if he only knew.

"I think you'd do better to be getting yourself ready for a trip to Manteo," he told her levelly when her voice ran down like an old wind-up Victrola.

She stared up at him blankly, then gathered herself together and asked with forced enthusiasm, "Manteo? Then you're going to work on it from that angle, too?"

"We'll need blood tests, licenses, and that sort of thing. I may be able to pull a few strings and speed up the process," he told her calmly, as if he were proposing a visit to the library for additional information.

They were married in a church that sat out on the beach. Wind whipped Emma's ivory dress of string crochet about her knees and threatened to sail her tiny hat out over the dunes as she left the small Methodist church beside the man who was now her husband. He held her arm as if afraid the wind would take her, too, as they spoke to the several people gathered outside under a clear, deep blue sky. Rain had come finally to wash away the lingering traces of August and the cobalt dome overhead promised an early autumn.

The church had been crowded with local people, most of whom claimed at least cousinship with Dan, and Dan had even managed to get Rosie down in time to serve as bridesmaid. Dennis was restrained in his role as ring-bearer, but his face was suffused with repressed excitement. Emma couldn't decide if it was their wedding, or the anticipated visit with the Pughs that was causing him such delight.

Hugh had given her away—a Hugh who had seemed sober to the point of nervousness—and Emma could only hope it was the occasion that had brought about his pale quietness instead of the affair with Derek.

Dan had forbidden her to even broach that matter with him and so she chatted with a spurious brightness about Ed and Treva's call the night before.

Anything and everything to keep her from thinking. She had done too much of that since that morning when Dan told her to get ready to go to Manteo.

She had thought he was joking at first; then she decided he was trying to teach her a lesson, and only at the very last did it dawn on her that he was entirely serious.

"I'm not in the habit of perjuring myself for anyone," he had told her when she demanded to know his reasons. "It suits me to acquire a wife and it suits you to acquire a husband." He had held up a staying hand when she opened her mouth to protest. "You won't be safe from that scum until you have someone who can stand up for you. Your father's not around, and from what your brother tells me your stepmother has him more or less hamstrung. Hugh's not man enough to protect you, although he may improve once you stop minding his business for him."

She had charged him with insulting her family, with meddling in her affairs, and anything else that flew to mind before subsiding. "But why should you do this for me?" she implored him.

"Let's just say I'm taking advantage of the circumstances, Emma," he told her enigmatically.

"You mean because of Margo?"

At first she thought he wasn't going to answer. Then, with a sardonic lift of one brow, he relented. "Partly. I told you I'd once asked Margo to marry me. That was twelve years ago. Three days before the ceremony was to have taken place, she got a hot tip and flew to Hanoi."

"But she came back?" Emma prompted, probing the painful subject as one would a troublesome tooth.

"She came back. And went off again and so on. You have to understand about Margo, Emma. We're sort of third generation friends, you might say. Her grandparents and mine lived here in Kinnakeet. Then, my folks moved away about the same time that Margo's parents were divorced. Her mother died not long after that, and Margo moved to Georgetown to be with her father and the two families sort of picked up again. Margo always hated the island . . . not enough scope for her ambitions, I guess."

Emma found it impossible to imagine Margo Summerlin as a towheaded, barefoot child, wading in the shallows with a boy who would have looked exactly like Dennis. Her eyes moved hungrily over Dan's profile.

"I guess I'm the closest thing Margo has to a brother . . . and in our case, there's a pretty hefty dose of sibling rivalry."

Dan might consider Margo in a sisterly light

now, but Emma was pretty certain that the feeling wasn't mutual. Margo's attitude toward Dan, while spiked with a certain malice, was decidedly possessive. Besides, he had admitted to proposing marriage, and that indicated something other than brotherly love.

There was so much more she wanted to ask him, so much more she needed to know for her own peace of mind, but for once, discretion prevailed and she left it alone.

She did say, though, that if the time came when Dan wanted to get out of their marriage, he had only to ask. It almost killed her to say it, but she had to be fair; he was doing this for her sake, no matter what polite excuses he made, and she was fool enough to grab at his offer with both hands. Like a gluttonous child in a candy shop, she smiled inwardly—feast now and pay later.

They returned to Larkin's Ridge after the brief ceremony and Emma assumed they would get on with the business of Reginald Fessenden, but Dan informed her they were leaving the next morning on a cruise in one of Field's boats for a short honeymoon. His lips had curled mockingly at the word and Emma had no need to remind him that in their case it was an empty term.

"We'll run down as far as Southport, probably, before heading back. Avon's a pretty small community with few secrets and I thought it as well to get out of the way so we could practice our 'yes, dears' and our tender glances in private."

"But that's not necessary, surely," Emma protested. They had stopped in the living room, and even though it was only just after four, Dan had poured himself a stiff drink and her the wine and soda she preferred. The small reception had been held before rather than after the ceremony and so the social pretense was done with, at least for the time being.

Dan's shoulders moved disparagingly. He had taken off the white linen jacket and now his tan silk shirt followed suit as he glanced noncommittally at his bride of a few minutes. "I prefer it. But for now, what say we head for the surf. The villagers will think we're crazy, of course, but they'll let us alone. I feel in the mood to wrestle half a dozen or so of the biggest flood-tide breakers—how about you?" His smiled disarmed her completely and she allowed herself to be pulled to her feet, forgetting she had stepped out of her shoes when she curled up with her drink on the rough linen-covered chesterfield.

"I'm game," she admitted, feeling ridiculously small beside him. When he smiled down at her and leaned over to place a kiss on her nose, she unconsciously lifted herself to her tiptoes and he raised his face and laughed at her.

"You are that," he declared indulgently. "About five feet nothing of pure up an' at 'em, aren't you?"

Chin lifting automatically, Emma corrected him. "Five feet and three-quarters of an inch and I've never lost a battle yet."

He whacked her on the bottom. *"Yet,"* he stressed softly. "Go on and change. Tonight I have something special to show you, but for now let's take advantage of a good surf. I noticed it through the church windows while I was waiting for you to join me at the altar."

"Dan Slater, you didn't, either," she laughed accusingly. "I don't think you can even see the surf from the church."

"All right, then let's just admit that I might have another reason for wanting to plunge into a cold surf and wear myself out."

She carried her blush to her bedroom with her and thankfully closed the door. That was something they hadn't covered, but it was going to have to be dealt with sooner or later, and this was a good way to postpone the discussion. Besides, what did she want?

Struggling into her suit, she admitted what she wanted. She wanted Dan Slater, every single aspect of him—his heart, his mind, his virile body. Her pulses quickened and her breathing grew shallow thinking about the last time he had held her and kissed her. Since asking—no, telling—her she was going to marry him, he had not touched her at all except for the brief peck at the altar and the casual kiss he had just dropped on her nose. But in the back of her mind, never allowing her to ignore it completely, was the idea that soon he'd be her husband, with all the rights and privileges that entailed. Did she want those rights exercised?

She knew she did. There were times when she couldn't think of anything but what it would be like to be carried in those arms to the very peak of fulfillment—but always in the back of her mind was the assumption that love would be the driving force, not mere lust.

She shook her head impatiently. The marriage was one of convenience for them both, although admittedly the benefit was largely hers. Who was to say that physical attraction hadn't played a part in propelling them into it? Dan certainly hadn't been able to hide the fact that he was aroused by her on more than one occasion, Margo or no Margo, and she . . . well, she knew her own heart and body were totally his for the asking.

Which was a demeaning position to be in. Maybe she'd just better play it cool, use that logic Treva had always declared would save her from ruining her life.

"The tide will be dead low if you don't hurry up, Mrs. Slater," Dan called through the door. "If you need any help, I'm yours to command."

Chameleonlike, the ocean reflected the deep blue of the sky, the waves smooth, with a ponderous driving force that surged to within fifty feet of shore before collapsing into a maelstrom of foam.

Feeling strangely on edge, Emma plunged headlong into the first crashing burst of surf and fought her way to the calmer waters beyond. Dan stayed with her, watching her with an almost smug indulgence that infuriated her for some perverse reason. The more he laughed at her daring, the more audaciously she launched herself onto the enormous waves, riding them all the way to the glistening gravelly sand, only to drag herself back up and slog out again.

It was unbelievably tiring and she admitted to herself that she was pushing it, running on pure adrenaline, but she couldn't seem to stop, not even when she caught sight of Dan's knowing grin. He kept up with her, holding himself in check as she waded out to where she could dive under the incomers and swim to deep water. He made no effort to support her now, despite the fact that she was in way over her head.

"One more, girl, and then we'll head for home, all right?"

"Make it a superchief," she challenged, hopping on the tip of one toe in the trough of the seas and rising to float over the top with her chin lifted high. It infuriated her that Dan seemed to hang suspended in the water no matter how deep it was, with no effort at all.

They waited in silent agreement until the third one out approached, readying themselves at the precise moment to take advantage of its force. Emma stroked and kicked for all she was worth, thrilling at the elevator sensation when she dropped from the crest to feel the full power of the thrust behind her.

They washed ashore, tumbling and laughing as their legs tangled together, and Dan helped her up, supporting her against his chest when she lurched drunkenly in reaction to the quicksand produced by the receding wave.

"Come on, Fearless Emma, time to go. Mrs. Pugh left a wedding supper for us that needs to be heated up, and the way I'm feeling now, I don't think I can hold out."

Later, she allowed the shower to stream over her head, quickening to the knowledge that just across the hall Dan was standing in an identical bath, feeling the stream cascading down on his head and shoulders. Was he thinking of her, too? Was he reminding himself that this was to be their wedding night?

Or was he only concerned with getting on with the wedding feast? Somehow her hunger seemed to have abated, and without the support of the buoyant salt water she was feeling strangely ennervated, not sleepy. Lord knows, sleep was the last thing on her mind, but for some reason, all the strength seemed to have drained out of her limbs, leaving her weak and trembling.

Afterward, she could never have said what it was they ate. She remembered only the burning intensity of Dan's eyes as he gleamed at her from across the table. He was amusing, charming, doing his best to put her at her ease, but as the hands of the brass ship's clock crept inexorably forward, Emma found herself almost paralyzed with anxiety. She drank three glasses of the deceptively smooth white wine Dan had produced and she was aware that *he* was aware of each time she refilled her glass. He didn't do it for her; he merely *looked* at her as her none-too-steady hand tipped the chilled bottle again and again.

Finally, he stood and pushed in his chair. "Let Mrs. Pugh deal with these in the morning. Now, it's time for that something special I promised you."

She felt the color fall from her face; actually felt it drain away and leave her staring, large eyed and trembling, at the man who waited for her to rise. He held out his hand, the smile on his lips relaxed and confident—all the things she wasn't—and she hated for him to know she wasn't taking the whole affair for granted, as he was.

"Well, I must say, you're awfully mysterious about it," she said with a brightness that didn't fool him for a minute. She stood, swayed, and put her hand in his, deciding discretion was the better part of valor under the circumstances.

The bride wore white and passed out immediately after the wedding supper, she thought to herself, and a giggle bubbled to her lips.

He led her to the center hall, from which the bedrooms, the baths, and the living room branched off in one direction, the kitchen and dining room in the other, forming a jigajag pattern that allowed double, and sometimes triple exposure, to most of the rooms. Overhead was an all-but-unnoticeable trapdoor and Dan caught at the chain and pulled it, opening the trap and at the same time lowering a ladder.

"After you, Mrs. Slater," he said suavely. "And for heaven's sake," he added a little impatiently, "take off those neck breakers!"

Meekly, she stepped out of her bone white shoes and tested the first rung.

He followed her up and braced the small of her back with a steadying hand as she caught her breath. They were in a room no more than eight by eight feet, with four windows on each side. There was a rush matting on the floor and a telescope mounted on a brass swivel base. That was all. No furniture of any kind. The light was a lantern suspended from a chain in the peaked center of the roof and Emma was drawn immediately to the windows.

Enthralled, she moved from one to the other, seeing the pattern of land against the Sound that reflected the last glimmer of light, but losing it altogether in the stygian blackness over the Atlantic. Lying low on the horizon was the aquamarine glow of light that pinpointed each village and closer beneath them warm incandescent squares revealed the placement of many of the houses, with glimmers from cars moving between them as if caught up in some silent quadrille.

"It's pure fairyland," she breathed, catching the omnipresent beam of the lighthouse with its own individual rhythm.

Dan remained silent but it was a warm, comfortable silence. She turned again to the ocean side, where only the occasional car passing by on highway 12 broke the velvety blackness.

"Keep watching," he urged her. "Within a few minutes you should begin to see a glow."

She was only too glad to obey, for in the closeness of the small space she was acutely aware of two things—Dan's nearness and all the wine she had consumed for dinner. She leaned her forehead against the cool pane of glass and waited. Down below, the light from the dining room window cast exotic shadows from a clump of palmettos, and when she raised her eyes again it was to see a faint, pearlescent gleam on the horizon.

Time seemed to hold its breath as the slow revelation began, and by the time the moon had climbed above the water to cast the glittering lure of its pathway out across the Atlantic Emma was utterly enthralled. It seemed perfectly right that Dan should slide an arm around her waist and pull her head onto his shoulder, but because she had left her shoes at the bottom of the stairway, her head only came halfway up. He turned her deftly and raised her face, smiling down at her in the shadowy dimness. "Like it?" he murmured.

"I love it."

"It was my mother's special place. The telescope was hers, left to her by her father."

She lifted her head from its resting place against his steadily throbbing chest. "I didn't know . . ." she began, then broke off in confusion when he laughed at her.

"That I had a mother? But what did you expect?"

"You've never mentioned her before."

He buried his face in the fragrant softness of her hair. "I built this place for her. She and Dad had planned it and then, when he died, I carried on with their plans. Mother lived here for almost three years—long enough to furnish the place— and then she died, too. I think this house they planned together must have been the last link with my father, and when it was completed, she lost interest. They had always been inseparable —still are, I suppose."

"I'm glad," Emma murmured. "I mean about your mother—that it was for her that you built the house, I mean," she blundered.

Dan lifted his head. "But who did you think . . . ? Oh. Margo."

And then it was as if the very mention of her name invoked the presence of the other woman, the woman Dan had once asked to marry him. "I think we'd better go back down, don't you?" he asked, leading her to the edge of the trapdoor and handing her down carefully.

Emma waited until he closed the door, her shoes in her hand, and then she sighed unconsciously. It had all been so lovely for a moment. All day, in fact—ever since she became Mr. Dan Slater. Now, with one word, the true situation was brought back to her unmistakably.

"I think if you don't mind I'll turn in, Dan," she said very politely. "The surfing—I'm suddenly worn out."

"Is it because I brought up—"

"No!" she interrupted. "It's only that I'm tired —I haven't gotten much sleep these past few nights." Her laugh was high and nervous and she hated herself for sounding like a self-conscious schoolgirl.

"You're sure . . . ?"

"Of course I'm sure, Dan! Why should Margo's name make any difference to me? I mean, after all, it's not as if this were a . . . a love match or anything. We both know it's merely a . . . a convenient arrangement for as long as . . . well, until one of us wants out."

Gone was the easy indulgence of the afternoon, gone the growing warmth that had penetrated her soul up on top of the world—until Margo had to go and interrupt them! Emma was as angry as if the other woman had physically come between them, and for all intents and purposes she had done just that.

It was late afternoon before they set out in Field's *Moonglow*, a sleek fiber-glass sports fisherman. The use of it for as long as a honeymoon as they cared to take was his wedding present to them. All her old optimism had risen through the day as she helped Dan close up Larkin's Ridge.

As Dan navigated Hatteras Inlet, Emma sat in the fighting chair and watched the crimson orb settle inexorably into the waters of the Sound. It almost seemed to hesitate just above the water and then it plunged with headlong relentlessness to disappear, leaving only a faint sigh of color to mark its going.

When it came to headlong plunges, she knew a thing or two, Emma observed silently. Behind her, Dan handled the boat just as effortlessly as he had handled everything else since Emma had known him. Had it only been a little over a month? Honestly, she had done some rash things in her life, but to marry a man she loved and then try to keep that love from him had to top the list.

For that matter, what if she were to let him know how she felt? He was attracted to her; she knew she had the power to arouse him, and perhaps that could lead to something more in time. What had she to lose except pride, and when you were alone pride could be awfully cold comfort.

She stretched out her legs to hook her feet over the transom and watched as Dan took them into the harbor at Ocracoke.

"We'll eat out tonight and tomorrow. On the way south you can try your hand in the galley," he called to her over the steady throb of the twin diesels.

While Dan was doing what needed doing to secure the *Moonglow*, Emma changed into a

soft, short chiffon dress that hung from spaghet-
ti straps and swirled lightly around her body,
caressing her sensuously. She had an idea it
might be a little much for a weeknight in Ocracoke, but never mind; the only man whose opinion of her mattered was now in the next cabin
getting changed to go out, and if he approved,
then the rest of the world could go hang.

He approved. It was in his eyes as they
gleamed appreciatively over her, dwelling on
the places where the soft, bias-cut material
clung to her rounded hips and the thrust of her
breasts. Her bronze sandals matched the black,
brown, and rust print of the dress and she flung
an airy stole of eggshell open-weave material
over her shoulders, avoiding the intensity of his
gaze.

The crisp, tucked-front white guayabera Dan
wore with white linen slacks brought out his
almost Mediterranean darkness, and for some
reason Emma was more shy of him than usual.
But as if he sensed this, he went out of his way to
put her at her ease.

Another meal went untasted as she rear-
ranged the scallops, the popcorn shrimp, and
salad on her plate. It seemed that each time she
raised her eyes they became entangled with his,
and when she didn't, it was only because her
glance never lifted above the tuft of dark hair
revealed at the open neck of his shirt.

"It might be interesting to bug your head
about now," he murmured as he refused the
waitress's offer of dessert.

"My . . . to bug my what?" she exclaimed,

jerking her attention back from the romantic fantasy that had been seducing her imagination.

"Bug . . . you know, as in electronic. I was just wondering what was responsible for the sunset colors that keep staining your face."

With a sudden easing of tension, they left, to wander slowly back to the *Moonglow*. Ocracoke was a delightful village scattered around the bowl-shaped harbor called Silver Lake. Its squatty white lighthouse rose over the inky darkness of oak and yaupon and the fragrant cedars. They were greeted by friendly voices in the darkness as they followed the narrow, winding road to the harbor.

A light breeze had sprung up after dark and it swirled Emma's skirt around her legs, giving rise to all sorts of strange sensations in her overheated mind. Dan's hand had caught up her own as they left the restaurant and they walked in harmonious silence until they came to the uneven wooden wharf. Then he swung her up in his arms.

"I should have thought of this on the way out. Who needs a wife with a broken leg? Those stilts you wear could prove fatal on these old planks."

With her breath coming in labored spurts, Emma told him to put her down—please! "Who needs a husband with a hernia?"

Throwing back his head, Dan laughed unrestrainedly. "And here I thought you might be feeling just a little bit self-conscious."

She was, only not in the way he meant. She was more conscious than ever in her life of the feel of her own body under the influence of his hands. The few scant layers of chiffon proved no barrier at all to the hard bite of his fingers on her sides and under her knees.

"We'll have a nightcap out here on deck," Dan murmured, his breath stirring tendrils of her hair against her neck. "Go climb into something —sorry about this—nautical but nice, and I'll mix something for us."

She groaned, burying her face in his throat. "You're dreadful!"

"It's nice to be appreciated," he returned smugly, setting her on her feet. He slid her down his body, steadying her for a moment before releasing her, and Emma felt the absence of his touch to the extent that she almost leaned against him once more.

Whoa, she cautioned herself, feeling her way below to the surprisingly luxurious cabin. Last chance for reason, logic, sanity, and all those other prime virtues that are supposed to make life so nice and orderly.

Too late, she answered herself, deciding that the wine must be talking, for she didn't usually indulge in such dialogs. Oh, much too late, thank goodness! She slipped the chiffon confection off and slithered into the second part of her four-piece trousseau—a caftan of silky thin cotton that drifted down about her bare feet in a cloud of moonlight gray. It was remarkably practical, she told herself piously, because the sleeves were proof against any possibility of chill and the flowing length would keep mosquitos from her ankles. She was rationalizing, babbling to herself like a silly adolescent, because she knew what she wanted to happen in the next hour. Hadn't the logic of the heart been overruling her head ever since she met the man?

Pausing to distill the moment, she wondered if realization could be that much greater than anticipation. The knowing that within a short time Dan would be making love to her gave her almost as much of a thrill as . . .

But how could she know that? Anyway, the whole idea was meaningless, because right now she was on top of the towering wave, being swept along on a breathtaking ride, and she could no more stop the course of events than she could stay the movement of the sea.

Dan greeted her silently, extending a tall glass of Cinzano and tonic water, and she found herself looking everywhere but at the commanding figure in the dark wraparound robe. He pulled her down beside him on a dew-wet cushion and left an arm draped almost casually across her shoulders as he gazed out over the pearly water of Silver Lake. Along the shore gnarled, whitened tree trunks loomed brightly against the night-black density of growth as the moon slipped out from the pearl-edged clouds. It was brilliant enough to cast a shadow and Emma felt Dan's eyes on her.

He took the untouched drink from her hand and placed it out of harm's way before turning her to him. "You look like a dryad in that thing you're wearing." His voice was a low, raspy burr against her nerves, raising the tension to almost unbearable heights. "But I suppose, under the circumstances, a naiad would be more like it. They'd have the same sort of eyes—tilted with mischief, shining with . . . what is it that's shining out of your eyes right now, darling?"

Her breath caught in her throat; it was the first time he had called her darling, the first time he had spoken an endearment of any kind to her, except for the rather condescending "little girl." It's love, Dan . . . I love you so much it frightens me, she wanted to say. She wanted to shout the words but she could only look at him helplessly, and then he stood and drew her to her feet.

The cabin was still hot with the heat of the day's sun but Emma didn't notice that. Dan left off the lights, allowing the moon to pour its silver through the portholes. When he lifted her, he held her close for just a moment, with the moonlight streaming over her features, and then laid her on the bed, following her after a brief pause in which his robe slid soundlessly to the floor.

"You're not afraid of me, are you, my little naiad? Don't be." His hands had moved over her shoulders to ease the caftan down and his fingers went unerringly to the few covered buttons that closed the front, as if he had memorized their position.

"No, Dan," she whispered, allowing her own hands to lift to his face. She held him there, even when she could feel him straining to lower his face to hers. Gazing into the shadow of his eyes, she willed him to commit himself to her, to utter some small hint of his feelings so that she could at least pretend he was taking her in love.

"I've waited too long for this, darling—since that first time I held you on the Ocracoke ferry when you invited the gulls to remove a succulent finger or two. My patience isn't exactly endless, you know." There was a thread of laughter in his voice, and he eluded her grasp and came in from the side to capture her mouth with his, settling against her in a way that made his state of arousal all too evident to her.

With impatience, yes, as well as a mastery that proclaimed his experience, he invaded the warm recesses of her mouth to trigger sensations that left her absolutely boneless. When at last he lifted his head, she faltered, "Dan, I . . . I . . ." Her whisper tapered off helplessly. She couldn't tell him. She hadn't the courage to give him the key to her heart when she wasn't certain he even wanted it.

"What is it, Emma? What are you trying to say?" His words drifted down to her softly, but it was his hands and what they were doing to her that rendered her all but mindless. "Then kiss me, darling. Show me what you can't put into words." He turned so that he was covering her with the weight of his body, pressing her into the firm support of the mattress so that she could hardly breathe, and when he realized it, he eased to one side again. "The spirit of you is as big as all outdoors, precious, and sometimes I forget what a small package you really are."

He had laid the silken fabric of her caftan open now and as her eyes adjusted to the moonlight, she could see his dark hands on the whiteness of her stomach. Somehow the sight of it affected her almost as much as the feel of him, and when he lowered his lips to tease the dusky peak of her breast, she groaned and pulled his head harder against her, as if wanting him to hear the words her heart was crying.

"Slater? You on board? Got a message for you."

The rough, careless voice ripped through the fabric of the night, doing irreparable damage as the *Moonglow* lurched to the weight of a third person on board.

Chapter Eight

An hour later, Emma curled up on a small portion of the wide bed and wondered why the last of August was suddenly so cold. Dan had gone almost immediately with the Coast Guardsman who had come for him, to be flown directly to Norfolk, where Dennis was in the hospital, suspected of having acute appendicitis. As the boy's guardian while his parents were out of the country, he had to get there as quickly as possible in case surgery was indicated, so there had been time for no more than a swift good-bye and instructions to wait aboard the *Moonglow* for someone to come for her.

It was almost eleven thirty when she heard someone hail her softly from the wharf and then the boat lurched as Field came aboard. Emma realized that, in spite of her conviction that she would never be able to sleep, she had been dozing. Now she sat up and buttoned her caftan and on an impulse wrapped Dan's robe around her as well.

"Emma? Field here. You awake?" Dan's cousin called from just outside her door.

They met in the narrow companionway, with Emma in her bare feet dwarfed by the big, blustering fisherman. "Sorry way to wind up a honeymoon, ain't it, honey?—but that kid means almost as much to ol' Dan as you do."

Luckily, the shaded light hid the stiffness of her smile from him and Field went about doing whatever he had to do to get underway.

"Go on back to sleep, Emma. I'll run 'er on up to Kinnakeet an' wake you when we get there so you can scoot on up to the house with nobody to ask dumb questions. Everybody knows the boy was took sick, but there ain't no need to make a soap opera out of it."

The lulling motion of the water, the muffled roar of the powerful diesels, and the unnatural apathy that had settled over her with Dan's leaving assured that she slept for most of the trip north. It was still dark, with that intensity that comes just before daybreak, when Field drove her to Larkin's Ridge.

By the time Dan called later on that morning she had got past the stage of self-pity and could react with proper concern to the news that Dennis was probably not going to have to have surgery, although he was still an awfully sick little boy.

"I'm glad, I can tell you, because I hate to

have the whole responsibility. Poor kid . . . he's hooked up to half the machinery in the hospital, but I really think he's on the mend."

"Oh, Dan, I'm so glad," Emma breathed. Then, in spite of all her resolutions to play it perfectly cool, she had to ask, "When are you coming home?"

"I'll stick around until Sara and Will get here. My sister, Dennis's mother. They should be in within a couple of days, depending on what sort of connections they could make."

Clutching the phone, Emma sank down on the bed, steeling herself not to reveal the depth of her disappointment. Foolishly, she had imagined he'd be just as anxious to get back to her as she was to have him here. Then, panicking lest he break the tenuous connection, she cried, "Dan?"

"Yes, Emma? Are you all right?"

"I . . . I'm glad he's going to be all right," she whispered. "Give him my love." And you, Dan . . . my love to you, too, she added silently, hanging up the receiver.

As soon as she put down the phone she was ashamed of herself. Of all the selfish, self-pitying, useless . . .

Impatiently, she jumped to her feet and went out to the kitchen. By the middle of the morning she had defrosted the refrigerator and cleaned the oven. She turned to the study next, but there was little she could do without Dan's supervision and so she wandered out into the back yard to stare down at the small boats.

Dan called again just before dark. "Still holding on, Emma?"

"Oh, yes, and you, Dan?" God, how inane it all sounded. Why couldn't she just come out with the words that were screaming to be said and let the chips fall where they would?

"He's enough better so that I might be able to bring him home after a couple more days. They've got beds out in the hall here—nobody malingers these days and gets away with it."

It was as if they were two polite strangers making conversation. "That's grand, Dan . . . I mean about bringing him home. Is there anything you need from here? What about your clothes and things?"

"I picked up enough stuff here to get me by for a couple of days and the hotel where I'm booked in has a pretty efficient cleaning service. Look, Emma, you can do me a favor and field any calls that come from the office. Tell 'em I'll call back, and if it's something that can't hold off, call me at this number and leave a message if I'm not there. I spend most of the time at the hospital, needless to say, but now that the boy's out of intensive care I'll have a few hours to sack up. Lord, I feel as if I hadn't slept in a month!"

After he had hung up, Emma stared at the torn envelope on which she had written down his number. She had the most terrible craving to call him back and keep him on the line. Somehow it all seemed real only when she could touch him or hear him or see him, and she was deathly afraid she was going to wake up and find that she had dreamed Dan Slater altogether. Only the fact that she was here in his house with his ring on her finger lent credence to the whole fantastic affair.

Mary came over and brought a local dish she called Hatteras-style drumfish, a mixture of boiled drum, potatoes, crispy little squares of fried salt pork with the briny drippings, and chopped raw onion. It was liberally laced with salt and pepper and she stood by and insisted that Emma eat at least a little of it, along with the delectable cornbread, still warm from the oven.

It didn't look any too promising, but Mary was watching expectantly and Emma had forgotten to eat during the day and so she forked up a bite.

To Mary's satisfaction, she finished the whole dish. In spite of a rather ordinary appearance, the meal had been delicious, and when Mary poured them both coffee and began talking about Dan as a young man, Emma relaxed for perhaps the first time since a concerned young Coast Guardsman had broken into her honeymoon.

At eleven she was ready for bed, wondering how she'd ever manage to sleep again, and without allowing herself time to think she dialed the number Dan had given her.

If he were out, then what harm was done. If he happened to be there she could ask after Dennis and tell him good night, both perfectly reasonable excuses for calling.

On the other hand, if he were there and asleep, perhaps for the first time in ages. . . .

She didn't have time to complete the thought when the phone was picked up and a familiar husky drawl came over the line. "Hello, Summerlin here. Who's calling?"

With a small, strangled sound Emma replaced

the phone in its cradle. Later she wondered why she had been so shocked, but for now she simply sat there, stunned and wounded. In spite of all the logical reasons she managed to come up with later for Margo to be in Dan's hotel room at that hour of the night, her intellect was no match for her emotions, and she felt all her doubts return to coalesce into one big ache in the pit of her stomach.

By morning she knew what she was going to do. Norfolk wasn't all that far away and she could simply turn up and announce that she was there to drive them back home. No need to mention her abortive phone call, no need to let Dan think her coming had anything to do with him. And as for Margo—well, she'd deal with that when she had to. After all, she *was* Mrs. Dan Slater, and Dan *had* sent Margo away after discovering she had lulled Emma into an intense sunburn by passing off her lotion as a sunscreen, according to Mary.

She dressed with extra care, choosing a softly tailored cotton shirtwaist in a pale lavender-blue and swirling her hair up to add precious inches. She had an instinctive idea she might need all the help she could get and she checked her image before leaving the house—very cool, very businesslike, very unemotional. Just the right note, in other words, to handle whatever met her at the hospital or the hotel.

She decided to try the hospital first, for, after all, she was primarily concerned about Dennis. She wasn't familiar with Norfolk, but with the help of a city map picked up on the outskirts she located the hospital. Before she was quite prepared for it, she found herself following the starched and swinging bottom of a brisk, friendly nurse.

The children's ward was noisy and seemingly disorganized, but then she had not much experience with hospitals. She was halfway down the hall when she stopped short. As if her internal radar told her where to look, her eyes swung unerringly to the waiting room where several people sat, either staring off into space or thumbing unseeingly through dog-eared magazines. Sharing a plastic sofa were Dan and Margo, and Margo's head was resting on Dan's shoulder, her knees drawn up beside her and her stocking feet tucked cozily under Dan's windbreaker.

Emma's breath stopped; her heart too, for all she knew. Margo's eyes were closed, but she was talking, the words meant obviously for Dan's ears, and he sat leaning over, eyes on the brown square hands clasped before him.

The frozen tableau engraved itself on Emma's eyes as she stood there for what seemed an eternity before the nurse came back to say impatiently, "Mrs. Slater, this way, please. Visiting hours will be over in a minute."

Dan looked up, Margo's eyes flew open, and Emma turned away and followed the nurse numbly down the corridor to a room where four boys of about the same age were making engine sounds as hands traced imaginary flight lines through the air. All but one, that is.

"Emma, did you really come to see me?" Dennis asked with heart-wrenching eagerness. He looked unnaturally pale and small under the crisp blue and white spread; the tubes Dan had mentioned were still very much in evidence.

"Hello, dear, and yes, I really did," she said softly, dropping down into the hard metal chair beside him.

"Cousin Field's going to take me out to Diamond Shoals when I get well. He promised me when he called last night, did you know that?"

She hadn't, but it was like the big, kindly man and she stretched stiff lips into a smile that flowed into her eyes and became real as she listened to the boy telling her about the pictures he planned to take of the marlin he was going to catch.

"I'm going to be home by the time the storm hits and I'm going to take pictures of it from the cupola and I may even send them to the *Coastland Times*," he finished proudly.

"What makes you think there's going to be a storm for you to take pictures of?" Emma teased as her hands automatically smoothed the bedspread over the tiny limbs.

"Goll-ee, don't you even know about it? It's a . . . a tropical depression, but Uncle Dan says it's going to be a hurricane by tonight and it's headed right up the coast like the big storms back when he was a little boy."

Unconsciously, Emma glanced out the window at the clear blue sky. Was that just the faintest skeining of cloud overhead or was it her overactive imagination? "Well, you'd better hurry up and get well, then, if you're going to help me get through a storm, honey. I don't know the first thing about them," she declared.

"Uncle Dan says every few years old Mother

Nature has to sweep the beach off 'cause people keep puttin' houses out where they hadn't ought to. He says if they built where the Indians built a few hundred years ago, they wouldn't get washed out," Dennis announced.

"But then you don't see too many teepees or wigwams around these days, either, do you, old man?" Dan asked from behind her, making every muscle in Emma's body tighten painfully. "Hello, Emma. You came to see how the patient is getting along?"

"Yes, I . . . I thought I might be able to drive you home in a day or so," she said with a brittle smile. Her eyes registered a mixture of doubt and hope as she gazed up the impressive length of him. Even now, with half a day's growth of beard on his stubborn chin and his dark slacks looking as if he had lived in them for a week, the man was impressive. He wore his inbred air of authority with an unconscious ease that commanded respect in any surroundings. She was aware of the two young nurses on the other side of the ward casting covetous looks at him.

"We'll take off for a spell now, Dennis, and I'll see you later, all right?" Dan said, completely ignoring her remark about driving them home.

"See you later, alligator, see you in the funny papers, see you . . ." Dennis's singsong voice followed them through the door and Emma turned to speak to her husband as soon as they left the room, but he urged her on, a firm grip on her arm.

She trotted down the corridor half a pace behind him, and when they reached the elevators she was silenced by the solemn, inward expressions of a dozen or so passengers. She stood in front of him, staring down at her high-heeled pumps, acutely aware of the feel of him against her back. Could this be the same man who had swung her up in his arms and leaped aboard a boat with her two nights ago? If she had to address him right now, she had the uncomfortable feeling she'd find herself calling him Mr. Slater. Probably adding a "sir" for good measure.

Just for an instant when they stepped outside the huge building she might have imagined herself back in Washington, but the impatient grip on her arm was enough to bring her back to the here and now. She cast a helpless look at the man who was hurrying her across the street, her mouth opened to protest his high-handedness.

"Save it," he ordered curtly. "Where are you parked?"

Once more, in the cramped space of her car she attempted to speak to him, to bring up the subject of . . .

Good Lord! What subject? Certainly not Dennis's health, for she had seen for herself his condition, and not their interrupted honeymoon. In a hundred years she couldn't bring herself to remind him that after all she was his bride. Then *what*?

Margo Summerlin. Only how could she ask him what he was doing cuddling his ex-girl friend in a waiting room and what about the call she had made to his hotel last night?

Oh, blast! There was obviously a lot to be talked out between the two of them, and Dan must realize it, too, from the way he was dragging her off to Lord knows where, but for the life of her, she didn't know what it was anymore.

From a bored desk clerk Dan collected a key and ushered her to the bank of elevators, where once more disinterested passengers stilled any questions or comments she might have made. Once inside the room, though, he turned to her, one hand pushing the thick, untidy hair from his forehead and the other resting against the back of his hip. He looked thoroughly weary and thoroughly out of sorts, as if she were just one more of a long line of unpleasant duties he had had to attend to. Emma wished with all her heart she had never succumbed to this harebrained scheme anyway!

"Well?" he growled.

Beneath the lavender-blue dress, now pathetically wilted, Emma moved her shoulders resignedly. "Well, what?"

"Well, what was the idea of coming to drive us back in that kiddy car of yours? Don't you have a grain of sense at all?"

Of all the possible grievances she could have dreamed up, this was the most ridiculous. "What do you mean?" she demanded, thoroughly exasperated.

He jerked away from her, rubbing a hand across the back of his neck. "Okay, I'll give you credit for good intentions, if that's what prompted you, but why couldn't you have waited where you were until I had time to deal with you?" he asked tiredly.

"To *deal* with me! To deal with *me*? Let me tell you something, Dan Slater, you don't have to deal with me at all! You just go right ahead and deal with . . . with Dennis and . . . and Margo Summerlin, but don't waste your time trying to deal with me because I don't need you!"

"Oh, stow it, will you? Look, Emma, I'm in no shape to discuss anything with you now. I haven't had more than an hour's total sleep since I left you and I'm doing my best to hang on here until Sara and Will get back, but that won't be until sometime tomorrow morning, at the earliest, so that means I'm on call until then."

Compunction drained the belligerence from her stance and she dropped down into a chair before she collapsed. She had slept, but at the moment she hardly felt any better than Dan looked.

For the first time, she glanced around her with dull curiosity. They were in what appeared to be a sitting room, with a bedroom off to one side and a bath off that, its gleaming impersonality mocking the seething emotions that coursed through her. The bland recipient of who knows how many confidences, this small suite. How many lovers had met and made up or broken apart here? Why should she assume that her own case was special just because she couldn't seem to see beyond the man who stood impatiently in front of her.

"I need some aspirin," he said suddenly, wheeling away to go into the whitely gleaming bathroom. He didn't shut the door and she saw him toss down three tablets and wash them back with water. Her eyes never left him. His shirt, coincidentally enough, was a blue not unlike her own dress and it brought out the warmth of his skin.

Nothing could hide the strain of the past few days, however, and when she looked closer she could see a grayness underlying his tan, a deepening of the lines that bracketed his grim mouth.

Emma stood restlessly as he returned and dropped down heavily into the room's one easy chair. He still hadn't looked at her—not directly —and when he lifted a hand to the back of his neck again, she moved without thinking to stand behind him, her own hands going to his shoulders. She began to knead the rock-hard flesh. If he had repulsed her she would have left immediately, but he actually leaned forward to allow her hands more freedom and she continued her ministrations while her mind raced back and forth like a rat in a maze.

She hadn't the faintest idea where she stood; she was as much at sea as she had been before, but one thing was certain—she loved this man with an abiding fierceness that made it imperative that she at least try to hold on to the little she had of him.

"Ahhhh, that helps," he muttered roughly. "You have good hands, Emma . . . small, but firm and gentle."

Her fingers were at work on his temples now, touching, soothing the pulse that flickered beneath the weathered skin, and she resisted the impulse to run them through the dark thickness of his hair.

"I think I might snatch an hour's rest if you'd man the phone for me," he told her. "I haven't dared risk it because I'm not sure I'd wake up for an earthquake if I once went under."

Taking her agreement for granted, he stood, stretched, and moved off in the direction of the bedroom without so much as a backward glance at where Emma still stood, feeling about as needed as an empty candy paper. She watched as he practically fell across the orange bedspread, noticing that it was already rumpled, as if he had tried to get some rest, if not some sleep, before.

Her watch had stopped; Lord knows when she had remembered to wind it, but there was an electric clock in a horrid early American frame on one wall and she noted the time. Restlessly, she stood and, without conscious intention on her part, found herself beside the bed staring down at the sleeping form of her husband. She frowned tenderly and slipped his shoes off, letting them fall to the carpet. There was something infinitely touching about the sight of Dan's face in sleep. A wife should know about things like this, the aching vulnerability of a sleeping man, but then she wasn't a wife, only a bride, and not even very much of a bride.

An hour, he had said. She eased herself onto the bed beside him, taking care not to disturb him, although he probably wouldn't stir if a locomotive ran through the room. The minutes marched past the clock and one of her hands strayed to his belt. Should she have loosened it? No, that was what they did for people in shock. She rubbed the softly gleaming leather and hooked a finger in his belt loop. His warmth registered, even from the distance of half a bed away, and she edged a little nearer, taking care not to move too abruptly.

There wasn't the slightest break in the deep, even breathing as he moved a leg to a more comfortable position, and she turned so that she could watch him, even reach out and touch his hair if she wanted to. He slept on his stomach with his head turned away from her so she felt quite safe. One of her hands drifted gently to rest against his tricep, curling around to embrace its firm warmth, and she eased closer to his side with her face coming to rest against him. She could inhale the essence of him from here—the sweat, the pine-scented soap he favored, and a hint of laundry detergent the maid or someone had used on his shirt. It was pleasant, exciting even, and she admitted to herself that she selfishly wanted him to wake up. Perhaps unconsciously her fingers tightened on the muscles of his arm, for he mumbled something under his breath and rolled over, practically crushing her before she could scuttle away.

He turned to face her and his eyes opened sleepily. He gazed down at her, surveying her completely from under half-closed lids before he murmured, "Who's minding the store?"

"I wasn't going to sleep," she assured him hastily, coloring under his frankly sensuous appraisal.

"Not tired?"

"No . . . not really," she admitted, wondering wildly what excuse she could give for climbing into bed with a man who only wanted a few minutes peaceful rest.

The warmth that had been generated by his sleeping body came to her in an intoxicating drift, the scent of him stronger now and very human, terribly exciting to her raw senses. It was impossible to look away, equally impossible to control the breath that was fluttering shallowly in her throat. With a feeling of inevitability she watched his hand reach out for her, drawing her those last few inches so that she rested against the length of his body. He tucked her face into his throat, giving rise to all sorts of liquifying sensations and his words drifted down to her as if in a dream.

"Mmmm, you smell like a flowering tree I remember climbing as a boy. What was it, I wonder? I remember I fell out of it and sprained my wrist. Could that be a warning, do you think?" His laughter was a thing felt instead of heard and it made all sorts of tremors run the length of her spine, causing her to nestle even closer to fit his aggressively masculine body.

With a hand rounding her hips, pressing her to him, his mouth trailed across her cheek to catch the point of her chin, his tongue reaming out the shallow dimple there before moving on to her lips. "Oh, Emma, Emma," he groaned against her mouth, making it open like a flower opens to the life-giving sun. He moved over her so that she was a captive to his weight, but this time he carefully protected her, bearing himself slightly to one side so that his own leg and arm took some of the strain.

His hands held her face, cradling the delicate bones of her jaw and then spreading up to shape her lips for his mouth. Shattering what little mind she had left with his kiss, he allowed one hand to journey the short, tantalizing course down to the buttons on her dress and he opened them, very slowly, very deliberately, still not lifting his mouth from hers.

"You've got on too many clothes, wife of mine," he groaned against her teeth, and he lifted himself up on one elbow to finish the job of untangling her clothing.

Feeling abandoned without his touch on every part of her body, Emma reached up to him, running her hands inside the neck of his shirt and then tugging it impatiently from his belt. She said his name, softly, tentatively, the words laden with meaning she wasn't ready yet to impart.

"This isn't the way I planned it, darling, but for obvious reasons, this is the way it's going to be. Why don't you climb out of all that unnecessary harness while I take a quick shower. I'd hate to tell you how long I've been living in this skin of mine."

When she came reluctantly off her side of the bed, Dan met her halfway, catching her as her knees almost buckled beneath her, holding her so that she was flamingly aware of his need of her.

"You're a tempting little package. You'd better get away from me before I move in and destroy all the pretty wrappings to get to what's inside," he whispered against her mouth while one hand sought the soft, sensitive flesh that was barely covered by her lacy bra. He drew his breath between his teeth and moved her against his body. "You see what I mean, sweetheart? Get thee behind me."

He put her from him abruptly and strode the few feet to the bath, closing the door behind him this time, and as Emma gradually came back to earth, she followed him with her eyes.

It was as if someone had slammed a fist into her solar plexus. There, still swinging gently on a hook on the door, was a familiar white silk dressing gown, the ecru lace cascading down the lapels in mocking flourishes.

Dimly, she could hear Dan's voice coming through the door as she automatically refastened the buttons of her dress with frozen fingers. She turned slowly to the mirror, staring with wide, strangely blank eyes at the flushed face, her lips still swollen from Dan's kisses. She twisted her hair up into some semblance of order and tucked the facing back into the neck of her dress—as if it really mattered—before picking up her purse and quietly letting herself out the door.

Sooner or later they might have to talk, if only to undo the terrible tangle they had made of three lives, but for now she had to get away—as far away as possible so that she could begin to forget Dan Slater, begin to forget the hateful sight of Margo's dressing gown hanging so casually on his bathroom door.

Chapter Nine

Blundering through the confusion of a strange city, Emma found herself halfway to Virginia Beach and then, retracing her route, she turned off too soon and discovered she was in the middle of something called Chesapeake. Fortunately, she was able to get onto Battlefield Boulevard, where an attendant at an information booth told her she could keep going and the Boulevard would turn into highway 168, taking her all the way to Nags Head in little more than an hour. From there she was home free.

Somewhere in the midst of the rich, alluvial farmlands of east Carolina it occurred to her to wonder why she was fleeing to Larkin's Ridge. Now that cool rationality had taken command of her actions once more, she was able to decide her course. With Dan tied up in Norfolk for the next day or so, at least, she'd be safe in stopping at least long enough to pack up her things. She could call Rosie from there and tell her . . . tell her what?

That much she would decide later. Right now she needed to get there, to have a private place where she could hole up and lick her wounds, could talk herself out of this morass of bewildered self-pity and then pick herself up again and start marching.

The drive seemed interminable, but at least she wasn't headed west, with the setting sun in her eyes. In fact, there didn't seem to be a setting sun at all today. Glancing in the rearview mirror, Emma saw the thick bands of heavy bellied clouds and she slowed automatically and peered curiously out both side windows.

The sun was only visible as an opalescent backdrop to sheets of small, regimented clouds. What was it they were called? She racked her brain, glad of an exercise that would take it away from the insoluble problem of her marriage, but she soon decided that nimbostratus and cumulonimbus were mumbo-jumbo to her.

It looked as if it were going to rain, though, and rain hard. She pressed harder on the accelerator as she approached Currituck Bridge, wondering if she had closed all the windows at the Ridge.

A radio might have been useful, but hers had been out of commission for months. She hadn't bothered to have it fixed, hoping to replace it with an FM one when she could afford it. Still, if there had been any danger of a hurricane, Dan would have warned her. Hadn't Dennis said it wasn't actually a hurricane yet?

Dismissing the niggling thought that anyone living twenty-four hours a day in a hospital might conceivably lose track of the days, she decided to check with Field as soon as she got to Avon. If she was needed to look after things at the house, then of course she'd stay, but if not, she'd be on her way north by morning.

The front door opened to her touch, causing her to wonder if she were even worse off than she had thought. Before she got as far as the living room, though, she was greeted by a small, round woman with a shiny red face under cropped gray hair. "You're Dan's Emma," she declared firmly, wiping her hands on a lurid apron with ruffles and rickrack abiding incongruously alongside palm trees and sailboats.

"And you're Martha," sighed Emma, knowing without having to think. She dropped her purse on the pine table as if it had suddenly grown too heavy to bear and then she burst into tears.

Two cups of coffee and a bowl of clam chowder later Emma showered and changed into her dark green slacks and Hugh's old shirt. She left her hair wrapped in a towel and went out to the kitchen to help Martha with whatever needed doing and they decided to have another bowl of the delectable chowder and some hot corn muffins for supper.

"Crackers won't be worth a toot in this weather," Martha declared. Emma had already discovered that the woman never simply said something, she made a pronouncement, but for all her brisk, brusk manner, she was a kind person. Emma was glad to have someone in the house to keep her from wallowing too deeply in a trough of self-pity.

It was raining now, a sullen, fitful sort of rain that flung itself against the black windowpanes and looked as if it might go on forever. Dennis's storm was now officially a hurricane named Clara and it was reported to be moving with unusual speed up the coast of northern Florida.

"Leastwise, the Gulf won't take a walloping this time. My sister lives in Mobile and the tales she has to tell! Nossir, this one's goin' to slam down on Hatteras Island just like they used to do when I was a girl. Many's the time I've come outten a sound sleep to see my folks puttin' stacks of old magazines under the furniture to keep the tide from ruining everything. Got so's I could tell how close it was by how often Pa got up to thump on the barometer."

They were washing the two bowls and Emma was munching on the last muffin with some of Martha's fig preserves on it. "Is this part of the storm? This rain? I plan to be leaving for Washington first thing in the morning," she said a little anxiously.

She had told Martha only that she had gone to Norfolk to see Dennis and that since she wasn't really needed there she had come back. The tears she had excused as being from mere tiredness, although she wasn't certain how successfully she had prevaricated. Martha had cuddled her like a baby, but there was a speculative look in her faded blue eyes after that, a sort of "if you say so" look.

"Washington!" the woman exclaimed now.

"You won't be traipsin' very far in this storm, not if I know my bunions. They can tell the fall of the pressure better'n any glass, and besides, Mr. Dan will be expectin' you to stay put till he can come tend to you himself."

Mr. Dan can tend to his own business, Emma bristled silently. She didn't want to argue, not with anyone who owed their loyalty to her husband, but Emma had no intention of hanging around here waiting while Dan made up his mind about what to do. Once more she saw the mocking sway of a silk negligee on his door in her mind and she felt like growling.

After the housekeeper retired, Emma called Rosie. There were things she could say to her friend that she wouldn't want Martha to hear, so she put off the call until quite late. She listened to the repeated ringing of the phone as she stared unseeingly at a branch that was beaten helplessly against the window by the rain.

"Hello, Rosie? It's me, Emma . . . I'm in Avon —where else? The storm? Well, it's raining like the thirty-ninth day, but other than that and a bit of wind. . . . No, it's too early yet, I'm sure, and . . . Dan? No, he's in Norfolk."

She told her everything—not that she had planned to, but once the finger came out of the crack the dam went. Besides, she would never have been able to put Rosie off with half-truths. According to Rosie, whenever Emma tried her hand at prevarication her voice grew thin and terribly cheerful and her eyes were like marbles, so she let it out and the other girl listened to the end without a single interruption.

"So I'm coming back, Rosie. Dan won't be

expecting to find me here when he gets back, and anyway, there's nothing to hang around for. It's all over. . . . Of course, I still owe him a whale of a lot of money. He paid off Hugh's gambling debt, but I can pay that back." She giggled, and the sound held a hint of wildness. "I could always pawn my rings to get the money."

"You finished?" Rosie asked dryly. "All right, now, you listen to me for a change. You married the man and he married you and you darned well owe it to each other to end it face to face. If you don't—if you just run out and leave it like that—then it'll start to fester and drag on and on and the first thing you know you'll be sick with it! You can't start healing up until you've lanced the thing and let the poison out."

"Hush, darn you," Emma laughed shakily. "You're making my marriage sound like a . . . like a boil! There's nothing to talk about, Rosie. He has no intention of giving up his . . . well, I can't say his fiancée, under the circumstances, so maybe his mistress would be the proper . . . or the improper, term." She sounded brisk and bright and so terribly blasé about the whole thing, just as if it weren't killing her by degrees.

"Well, that's between the two of you, but Emma . . . you can't move in here either."

"I can't . . . !"

"I meant to tell you when you got back from your honeymoon. I've got another roommate." There was an extended silence during which the lines crackled alarmingly. Then Rosie broke in defensively, "Well, what did you expect? I mean, after all, you were married and all and . . . well,

I packed away your things and they're here for you whenever you get up this way. Twice I've stumbled over that trunk of yours, Emma, so . . ."

"But, Rosie," Emma wailed. Then, getting a hold on herself, she admitted that her friend had every right to fill the vacancy. It hadn't occurred to her even to wonder what she was going to do about the vacancy and the other half of the rent. In a calmer tone: "Did your sister decide to give city life a try after all?"

"No. Ah . . . as a matter of fact, Hugh's moved in."

Dead, ringing silence. Then: "Emma? Did you hear me?"

"Oh, yes, I heard you all right, only I'm not sure I heard you." Emma laughed a little breathlessly. "Care to tell me what's going on between the two of you?"

"Just about what you'd expect to go on between the two of us," the other girl affirmed with a note of bravado. "I've been crazy about your brother ever since he first came to see you—he was carrying that box of books for you, remember, and I knocked a vase of flowers off and broke it trying to make room for him to put it down. He—well, let's face it, when it comes to looks, I'm no match for you, but . . . well, Hugh and I understand each other, so don't be surprised to get yourself a sister one of these days. We're seriously considering it."

They talked a few more minutes, but for the life of her, after she hung up Emma couldn't remember a word they said.

Hugh and Rosie! Hugh and Rosie? Well, why

not? It might be the best thing that could happen
for either of them, and if they were happy, then
who was she to dash cold water over their
dreams?

It was still raining when Emma opened her
eyes the next morning. Martha bustled in with a
cup of coffee and Emma protested as she
stretched her arms up over her head and then
sat up, yawning. "Why do I always get sleepy
when it rains?" she asked with a good-morning
smile.

Ignoring her pleasantry, Martha informed her
that Field had already been by for extra clothes
and Dan's four-wheel-drive vehicle. "He's going
to drive it up to Norfolk before the highway goes
under."

Alarmed out of her muzzy-headedness, Emma
exclaimed, "Is that likely?"

"Fair certainty 'fore it's over. Radio says the
storm's stalled off the north Georgia coast.
Ninety-mile winds, so it's not too bad a one, but
when they stalls like that they usually pick up
considerable before they get to movin' again.
'Course, she could go to sea. Just have to wait it
out and see what happens. Drink up now and
come help me with the storm blinds.

The next few hours were too busy to give
much time for introspection as Emma followed
Martha's orders and closed the gray-green shutters. When she asked about the windows in the
cupola, the housekeeper shook her head and
declared that she was not about to climb that
fool ladder and hitch them things up.

With careful instructions, Emma climbed up

to the small square room and imagined she could feel the house shaking under the blast of wind and rain. Of course, this wasn't a hurricane—at least, not yet—but all the same, she could see water being driven in under the windows that looked out toward Hatteras. She stuffed the towels Martha had given her on the sill and closed the shutters on all the other three sides before tackling those where the wind was the worse.

By the time she descended the ladder again the small, round woman was frowning up at her worriedly, her hands clasped under the ruffled palm-tree-and-sailboat-print apron. "You set them hooks good, didn't ye? I'd hate to have one o' them shutters tear loose and come through the roof."

They got half a dozen or so pots from the kitchen to put under the leaks and when Emma expressed surprise that a house this new had leaks, Martha uttered her thoughts about a man who'd design a house with "more roof joints than a snake has apples an' a leak in ever' one of 'em!"

Emma didn't even try to interpret that metaphor, especially since almost immediately after that the phone rang. Martha announced after hanging it up that she was going to sit out the weather with her sister's boy now that Emma was there to look after Mr. Dan's house.

"But Martha, I don't know the first thing about storms," Emma wailed.

"Nothin' to know but to keep your head and open the offside windows," which had to be explained. "Pressure builds up in a house when the barometer is droppin' so fast outside an' it's best to let it out. Wind'll keep switchin' on you, too, so keep abreast of the windows and keep them pots emptied and you'll be all right. I've run enough water to get you through the next few days and there's food enough . . . candles in the pantry and a good Coleman, too."

"But what about tide?"

"Probably be some. Field took care o' the boats, along with his'n, but you don't have to worry none about high water. This house is on the highest place between Kinnakeet an' Buxton, an' even if it floated off the foundation, you'd not come to no harm long's you keep your wits about you."

Watching the rotund figure bundled up in a bright yellow slicker, a sou'wester, and shiny black boots, Emma thought hysterically that if she had kept her wits about her in the first place, she wouldn't even be here in the second place.

"What's his name?" she called after the housekeeper over the almost human moan of the wind. "Your nephew! I might need to call you!"

"Like as not the phones is already out. They'll go and then the power, if not the other way around," Martha dismissed with a wave over her head as she disappeared into the solid wall of rain.

She was wrong, though. While Emma stood there looking out despairingly at the scrub oak, whose branches seemed to drag the ground with the force of the screaming, wind-driven rain behind them, the phone rang once more, its shrill summons somehow chilling in the empty house.

It was Margo, and it was all Emma could do not to slam down the receiver, but she forced herself to be polite and noncommittal.

"You left so soon I didn't get to see you again, Emma. We were planning to take you out to dinner to this place that serves marvelous Chinese food that Dan and I discovered . . ."

"You didn't call to tell about the restaurants in Norfolk, I suppose, so why don't you say what's on your mind before the phone goes out. There's a storm here, you know." Margo seemed a thousand miles away, for some reason—hardly a threat to her anymore.

"Oh, yes . . . well, here's really what I called about. Dan asked me to tell you if you were still there not to wait for him. He'll probably run up to Washington for a few days and then we may fly over to Sicily. Sara—Dan's sister, you know—got in this morning and they'd rented a villa for the month and Dan and I thought we may as well use the rest of their time up, since they'll be taking care of Dennis."

Utterly numb by now, Emma was able to ask after the child and express delight that he was to be released tomorrow, barring complications.

"Oh, you'll never guess what!" Margo caroled, just as if the wind outside wasn't trying to lift the roof from the house. "I finally remembered where I'd seen you before. Dan and I were going over some Halpern clippings—oh, you'll be delighted to know we did the interview and it'll be a scoop. Well, anyway, there on the back of one of them was this picture of the antidraft demonstration outside the Heller Plaza and guess who was right in the middle of it? I didn't know you were mixed up with that Villers character, Emma. Did you know he'd just been indicted for . . ."

But Emma no longer cared. She hung up the receiver slowly, and if Margo wanted to think the lines had gone down, then let her. Only the realization of what Dan would think, seeing that picture with the policemen in the foreground and the angry, shouting mob on the sidelines, the sinking feeling that he wouldn't understand at all that she hadn't been involved, made her aware that she had still entertained a glimmer of hope.

Oh, yes you did, Emma Tamplin, she whispered as she slumped into one of the porch chairs that was now crowded into the living room. You stayed on here—you came back in the first place hoping he'd follow you and explain away that cursed negligee in his hotel room.

Well, you were wrong. He didn't come after you and he didn't call because he was too busy taking Margo out to Chinese restaurants and laughing at old news photos that should never have been printed in the first place!

She could see them now, relaxing in the sitting room of his suite, or maybe propped up in bed, papers rumpled cozily around them and cups of half-finished coffee growing cold as they chatted intimately. Margo would lean over and laugh, saying, "Oh, look at this one, darling— here's your little secretary coming out of a hotel with Villers and some other man. I *knew* I'd seen that face before. Hmmm . . . now what could they have been up to?"

And Dan—what would Dan do? Would he

laugh, too, and then drop the clipping to turn to the woman beside him for something other than laughter?

Oh, what difference did it all make now? He'd soon be in Sicily with Margo and he wouldn't be laughing at her *then*—he wouldn't even *remember* her!

Oh, you maudlin, stupid fool, you! Emma jumped up and paced across to stare out into the unnatural darkness. Then, on impulse, she hurried to her room and dragged out her two suitcases. With the drawers of clothing pulled open, she left and dashed back to the phone to call Mary.

"Mary, this is . . . yes, it is, isn't it? I've never experienced one before. Listen, Mary, is Field back by any chance?"

She learned that Mary wasn't expecting her husband back, and therefore Dan either, until the worst of the storm was over, although the four-wheel-drive vehicle was high enough to make the trip in all but the most extreme conditions—that is, if one had no better sense than to attempt it.

"But the tide isn't up yet, is it?" Emma pleaded frantically. To be trapped here suddenly seemed the very worst possible fate, and it wasn't the storm that frightened her.

"Must not be. They're still telling folks to evacuate—not that any of my family, nor Dan's either, has ever run from a storm. But then, we don't live in a shoebox perched up on stilts on the surf."

Ascertaining that once Larkin's Ridge was battened down there was very little to do except

wait it out, Emma said she'd better go and empty
the pots under the leaks one last time.

"Emma Slater, you're not thinkin' of doin'
something stupid, are you?" Mary demanded
suspiciously.

"Lord, no, Mary. My stupid days are behind
me, I sincerely hope." Emma laughed ambigu-
ously, saying good-bye and putting down the
phone just as the line crackled ominously.

Within ten minutes she was on the road—and
wondering with a sinking heart how she was
going to be able to see where she was going. With
the rain coming down in horizontal sheets and
the highway disappearing under enormous
black puddles that could be three inches or three
feet deep, she was forced to creep along. Her
hopes of getting off the island before the force of
the storm struck were diminishing by the minute.

There was practically no traffic on the roads
and what there was were high trucks or four-
wheeled beach vehicles. Emma felt terribly vulnerable in her small blue Pinto. The windshield
wipers were making her dizzy with their ineffec-
tive action and she fumbled for a tissue and tried
to wipe away the cloudy moisture on the inside.

Just north of Rodanthe the highway appeared
high and clear as far ahead as she could see and
the rain seemed to have slacked off a bit. Sitting
up straighter, she cracked a window to allow the
steam inside the hot interior to dissipate, then
swore roundly when she hit another patch of
water.

The car felt as if it lifted off the highway as she
braked and began to creep along. Just as she

muttered a prayer of thanks that for the most part the roads were straight, she saw headlights coming at her, headlights that rainbowed blindingly on her windshield, causing her to practically slow to a stop.

It was awful! Her fingers clamped so tight on the steering wheel that she had to lift them one at a time to get the circulation going again. She felt like screaming from pure tension as she inched along blindly, unable to see with the rain and the darkness and the haloed headlights of the oncoming vehicle. There was no indication at all of where the edges of the highway were and she could only trust her sense of direction not to run her off into the soft, flooded shoulders.

The other car crept past at almost a standstill speed and Emma concentrated for all she was worth on not being blinded by the lights. Once it was past, things were somewhat better, but she was still in water several inches deep and forced to move along at less than five miles an hour.

Something caught her attention and she spared a glance for her rearview mirror. Red lights . . . white lights . . . ?

It was backing up. The car she had just passed was reversing almost as fast as she was going forward and she had an instant vision of an enormous tidal wave bearing down on them.

She stopped. If the other driver was reversing, it could be because he had the latest bulletin on the storm and she needed to know. She waited, watching the uncannily straight progress of the other vehicle. When it got closer she could see a head hanging out the side, the door propped open, and she opened her own window to hear whatever it was the driver needed to tell her.

"Get out!" he shouted above the wind.

"What?"

"I said get out, you stupid fool!" The man swung down out of the shiny square-looking vehicle and she caught her breath in disbelief.

"I'm not . . ." she began, and then he was in beside her, shoving her across the seat and reaching in the back for her bags.

"Get out," Dan ordered tersely. "I'm driving you back to the Ridge and Field will bring your car—that is, if he can make it. Any fool who'll set out in the middle of the night with a hurricane on top of them deserves to be left to the devil, but I'd never . . ." He broke off impatiently. Even in the darkness, Emma was aware of an anger that overshadowed anything the puny forces of nature could manufacture.

Chapter Ten

They followed Field in her car as far as they could and then, when the water got too deep, they left the car and Field climbed into the steamy cab with them. Emma could do no more than smile weakly at him. She and Dan had not exchanged a single word since he had more or less thrown her into the cab. Both men were intent on divining the course of the highway under the impenetrable black water that by now completely covered it.

They took Field home first and he didn't even suggest that they come in. Emma would have gone willingly. In fact, she made a move to follow him only to have Dan latch on to her shoulder and haul her back in no uncertain terms.

He left her bags in the car. They were wet, for the windows had had to be open to see and rain had blown in all the way back. Emma was wet, too, shivering with something more than cold, but Dan ushered her inside with no more pity for her condition than he would have shown a fugitive from the law.

"Power's still on, so how about making a big pot of coffee?" he barked without once glancing at her. He was busy doing something to a flashlight and then he disappeared into the utility room and emerged with two lanterns. "The coffee?" he reminded her with mock patience.

Emma put the water on to boil and then she went to her room, peeling off the sodden garments as she went. Not until she started the steaming water to gushing into the tub did it occur to her that she had nothing dry to put on.

Before she could make up her mind what to do about it, Dan pushed open her door and dumped her bags inside, scarcely glancing at her before disappearing again. Standing in the middle of the floor in her soaking wet slacks and her nylon bra, Emma almost exploded with anger.

How could he be such a . . . a . . . words failed her. And she had thought she loved the man! Well, she was out of danger now, thank you very much, and it would be a cold day in July before she succumbed to those hot, ebony eyes and that flashing white grin. He acted as if she weren't even here, and it had been *he* who had dragged *her* back by brute force.

She marched out into the hallway, intent on telling him just what she thought of him, and then she marched right back again and turned off the hot water just as it reached the top of the tub.

Disheartened, she sat down on the edge of the yellow bathtub and stared at her bare feet. Her toes were white and slightly shriveled from wearing wet shoes for so long, but it wasn't her own condition that was prying into her consciousness like a worm in an apple—it was Dan, and why he was back here. Why he had stopped her when by all rights he should have cheered her off the island.

She sat there, her mind fumbling through the impossible situation while she drained out enough water, and then she finished undressing and lowered herself thoughtfully into the tub. From time to time she could hear hammering and she heard Dan's footsteps overhead. He must have wondered if anyone had secured the cupola.

She was dressed in a dry pair of slacks and a pullover sweater, sitting disconsolately on the side of her bed when Dan entered again. Without bothering to knock, she noticed indignantly, casting him a speaking glance from under the weight of her half-dry hair.

"Your coffee." He placed the cup on the table beside her and stepped back, leveling a look at her that took in everything about her appearance, from her bare feet, to the white duck pants and the peach-colored pullover, to her scrubbed face.

No doubt she didn't stack up very high when he held her up against the sort who wore designer clothes and . . . and white silk negligees. "Well?" she challenged, weary of being on the defensive for so long.

"Well?" he repeated infuriatingly.

"Why did you bring me back here? I was going home!"

"You *are* home, Emma. Make no mistake about that," he informed her dangerously.

She couldn't drag her eyes away from his mouth. It looked so grim, the bracketing lines beside it deeper and grayer than ever, as if he hadn't slept since she left him in Norfolk. "No I'm not, Dan. I'm at your house . . . not mine. There's nothing here for me and we both know it, so why drag things out any longer. You made a gentlemanly agreement—a gesture that saved my skin—and I thank you for it, but . . ."

He slashed through her words angrily. "You thank me for it. You *thank* me! Why, you sanctimonious little hypocrite! You sit there mouthing polite little inanities about gentlemanly gestures, when . . ." He broke off and reached for her, jerking her up by her arm. "I'll give you an example of a gentlemanly gesture and then you'll have something to thank me for! You can take this with you when you hit the road again!"

His face went swiftly out of focus as her frightened eyes were shadowed by his lowering features. His mouth struck hers in a hard, cruel kiss that wrenched her lips apart and plundered ruthlessly all she would have gladly given.

Everything faded away—the shrieking wind, the rain that drove against the walls with shuddering force, and the familiar room—as he lowered her down to the bed and followed her with the full weight of his body. No tender concern now for her diminutive size. Rough hands pulled the sweater from her body, flinging her arms aside and then her pants went. He fumbled at his own clothes.

"Dan, no! You can't do this!"

"Can't I, Emma?" he growled, lowering his body to cover her own.

She could feel the thunder of his heart, as if the very forces of the hurricane were inside him screaming to get out. Then his lips found her temple, and the hollow beneath her cheekbone, dragging kisses across her skin through the moisture of tears she was unaware of having shed.

The eye of the hurricane—a stillness that transcended all that had gone before it as Dan's furious assault drained away in the sound of one word. "Emma," he groaned, dropping his face to her breast. "Ah, little one, what am I doing to you?" He lifted himself away, bringing in a rush of cool air that chilled her to the very heart. "Emma," he whispered again, and then he stood up and stared down at her, the anguish on his face clearly revealed in the light that suddenly flickered and then went out.

It was as if nothing had happened. Neither of them moved, and as far as Emma was concerned, all the endless darkness in the world could never wipe out the sight of Dan's wretched face, that magnificent body trembling as if it were one of the stout oaks, made vulnerable to the storm.

He touched her, a soft, tentative hand laid on the side of her face, and then his fingers traced the wetness down her cheek and she felt the springs give under his weight as he sat down beside her. "Emma, why were you leaving me?" he asked, his voice nothing like the stricken groan, nor the implacable coolness of before.

She couldn't *not* answer him. "I couldn't bear to see you again," she told him simply, lying there in the impenetrable darkness with his hand resting on her throat where it had slipped.

The whistle of his breath as it was drawn forcefully through his teeth cut through the air like a knife. "You don't pull your punches, do you?" His fingers on her skin curled up into a fist and she could feel the tension in him as it invaded her own body.

Her eyes widened. "Dan . . . no. It's not what you're thinking." She turned away from him, but only to bring the chaos of her emotions into focus so that she could explain to him . . .

Explain what? What could be said between them after all the confusion, the misunderstandings . . . the pain inflicted, the pain born? "Dan, I had to get away, to try and stop the . . . the hurting. When Margo called and told me . . ."

She was not allowed to finish. His hands caught her and turned her back toward him and he leaned closer so that she felt the heat of his breath on her skin. "Margo told you what?" he demanded roughly.

His fingers were biting into her flesh and she must have flinched, for immediately the grasp lightened. Then he lifted her and she found herself lying across his lap, her head cradled in the hollow of his shoulder. "Margo told you what?" he repeated softly, firmly. There was an underlying anger in his voice that belied the gentle pressure of his hands as they stroked her to where her hip rested on his hair-roughened thigh.

Under the comforting veil of darkness she told him of Margo's call, saying the words as if they were unrelated to the agony that had driven her out into the storm. "And that's why I went, Dan. You certainly didn't need me anymore." She took another gulping breath and continued. "I . . . I thought I'd get in touch . . . leave word where you could reach me when you got back and . . . and we could see about the annulment."

"An annulment won't be possible," he murmured against her hair.

She twisted her head around as if her eyes could penetrate the darkness and discern the meaning of his words. He took advantage of it to kiss her again, a tender kiss that threatened to get out of hand almost immediately as she felt the quickening of his body beneath her and found her own senses clamoring in response.

"No," he groaned against the softness of her mouth, "not yet." He lifted his face and eased her slightly away from him as if he couldn't trust himself to be closer, and then he began to speak. "Darling, we're going to defuse that particular bomb right now and then it will never have the power to hurt us again. I told you I had asked Margo to marry me twelve years ago. I was twenty-four then, and disgustingly idealistic!" His lip curved in self-derision. "It was the sort of summer when common sense flies out the window—you find yourself seeing everything from a crazy new angle. After years of merely accepting each other, warts and all, Margo and I suddenly found ourselves having an affair. All it took was a party, a few too many drinks, and when everyone else left, a full moon and an empty cottage on the Chesapeake."

Emma's hand, tucked in the opening of his shirt, curled into a small, tight fist. Suddenly, it even hurt to breathe.

Dan's voice, surprisingly emotionless, overrode that pain as he went on to say, "Like the callow youth I was, I did the gentlemanly thing and offered marriage." He laughed shortly. "Only by the time the date was set, I was pretty certain that if every man thought as I did Margo would have been up on bigamy charges. The parents were pretty well shattered when she walked out three days before the ceremony, but believe me, I knew what a narrow escape I'd had. I put a lot of energy into avoiding similar dangers from then on—had it down to a fine art, this business of uninvolvement." The mocking note in his voice brought Emma's eyes flying open to stare up at the thrust of his jaw. It had evidently been some time since he had last shaved, and he looked aggressively forbidding for a man who was holding her so tenderly.

It was the tenderness in his arms, not the grim thrust of his jaw, that gave her the nerve to ask, "But you still . . . she still . . . I mean, you invited her to spend her vacation here."

The arms tightened about her and suddenly the jaw above her didn't look quite so forbidding. "Honey, she needed me. In spite of everything, I'm still the nearest thing to a brother Margo has, and when she ran into a really bad stretch, she had nowhere else to turn. One of her reliable sources turned out not to be so reliable and she brought down a lawsuit on the network. In the middle of that, her father had a fatal coronary early this summer. The whole thing was too much for her and when she called and asked if she could come down here and hide out for a while, what could I say?"

What, indeed? Emma felt a sinking sensation as she envisioned a series of calls for help through the years ahead. And Dan would be there for her—he was that sort of man. Which was one of the reasons she loved him so desperately.

The sinking sensation dissipated slightly when he went on to say that he now had his doubts about Margo's reason for wanting to be here at this particular time. "I should have suspected something. Margo's never had any great love for this place. The lawsuit was settled out of court, but I'm afraid she's blown it again with this Halperson interview—at any rate, she's blown any friendship we once had by the way she tried to get rid of you once she realized how I felt about you."

Emma's head bobbed up and her fingers curled around the lapels of his shirt as she searched his features with imploring eyes. "How *do* you feel, Dan?" He had been absently stroking her thigh and now the tantalizing movement of his hand ceased.

"Good Lord, woman, what have I been trying to tell you all this time?" he exploded.

"That you're not in love with Margo. But that doesn't mean that . . ."

"That I love you?" He came as close to looking ill at ease as she had ever seen him—as if the word *love* had an unfamiliar taste on his tongue. "Yes . . . well . . . I'm afraid I'm not a very romantic man when it comes to flowery declarations—but Emma . . . don't ever put me through an ordeal like the one I've barely survived these past twenty-four hours."

"Dan . . . do you?"

He gathered her against his hard body as if he'd never get enough of holding her close. "I love you until I'm clean out of my mind with it," he groaned. "When you showed up at the hospital, I wasn't ready to admit it—not even to myself. I'd put in too many years convincing myself that I'd punctured that particular myth twelve years ago. I was so sure—" he laughed, and the sound of it brought tears to sting her eyes. "So dead certain that I had only the most impersonal, altruistic reasons for tying you to me with marriage. You needed help in shaking Villers and I'd already decided I'd seen enough of poor Margo to last me a lifetime. You were supposed to keep her off my neck. Margo can be pretty possessive in a dog-in-the-manger way, but not even she would consider barging into a brand new marriage," he reasoned bitterly.

"Only it didn't work that way," Emma murmured, fingering her way through the buttons on his shirt to tug at the dark hair that grew there.

"Only it didn't work that way," he sighed. Beneath her fingers, the beat of his heart was rapidly turning to thunder.

"You're darned right it didn't! When I saw you two canoodling in the hospital waiting room and then found Margo's clothes all over your hotel room—"

He nipped her ear in gentle punishment. "I'm not too sure of your definition of canoodling, but what she was actually doing was trying to talk me into using my influence with a certain politician to get her into a closed hearing. Margo's not above using her so-called womanly wiles to get her way. And she did *not* have her clothes scattered all over my hotel room, you suspicious wench! That bathrobe—"

"Bathrobe, huh! When they're pure silk, trimmed with handmade lace, they're not bathrobes, they're negligees!"

He grinned at her as his hands began to make daring forays of their own. "We'll have to go shopping for a trousseau for you, won't we? Do you suppose we could find something like that in the children's department? I'd hate to have my bride trip on her skirttail and break her neck." He tilted her head to bury his face in that particular part of her anatomy, setting off a frantic stampede of her pulses.

"You can't get out of trouble by insulting my size," she stated firmly—only the firmness was not very convincing when she was trembling from head to toe with the sensations that were coursing through her.

"All right, love, let's clear away all this business about Margo and get on to more important matters. Margo called from Richmond to say she needed to talk to me about something terribly important. I had no idea where I'd be at any given time, so I arranged with the hotel for her to get my key and told her I'd either be there or at the hospital. She tried the hotel first, and as I wasn't there, she made herself at home. Maybe the negligee thing was a ploy—I don't know. Perhaps it was supposed to trigger my libido, but to tell you the truth, I never even noticed the blasted thing. I suppose Margo freshened up and girded herself for battle, then she tackled me at the hospital—when you, unfortunately, saw us and came to your own conclusions. Then, back at the hotel, you turned me inside out and then ran out on me—I could have wrung your neck for that, sweetheart. But before I could take off after you, Sara called, then the hospital called, and I couldn't get away to catch you. That, my sweet pint-sized Amazon, was when I knew I had had it. No man goes through what I went through unless he's head over heels in love."

"I thought you weren't interested in catching me—if I thought at all. Mostly I just hurt. Oh, Dan, I've never hurt so much in my life!—except when Margo called to say the two of you were going to use up the rest of your sister's Italian vacation and I was free to go back to Washington."

He stiffened so suddenly that she was nearly dumped off his lap. "She *what*?" There followed a stream of succinct profanity that told Emma she had nothing to fear from that particular source again. "It's not the first time she's tried to get her way with an outright lie, but it'll be the last, as far as I'm concerned. I promise you that!"

"Dan, why couldn't you just tell me that you loved me?"

He stood up with her in his arms and lowered

her carefully onto the bed, following her to take her face between his hands. "I told you, I didn't even know what ailed me until it was too late. I went down like I'd been poleaxed once it hit me, but you were long gone by then." He began the slow, delicious process of undressing her. "Why couldn't you just trust me, my little love?"

The lights chose that moment to flicker back on and she caught her breath at what she saw in his eyes. "I—the clipping. I though you'd probably . . ."

He laughed aloud and she could see her own reflection in his warm, dark eyes. "That thing? Good Lord, woman, I'm in the newspaper business. Don't you think I have sense enough to evaluate a thing like that? Margo showed it to me and offered her own interpretation, but don't forget I knew about Villers and your stepbrother. It didn't take much in the way of analysis to put that little item where it belonged—in the trash." He touched the corner of her mouth with a quick, exploring tongue. "Hmmm . . . you really are photogenic, though. Shame there's not enough of you to go in for a modeling career."

His finger drew a line from the shallow dimple on her chin down her throat to her breast, where the dusky bud of her nipple bloomed at his sensuous touch. "You mean you want to put me to work?" she managed to whisper, her hand busy divesting him of his shirt.

"You're coming right along as a research assistant, but I have other plans for your immediate future." He shucked the last of her clothes off and stood up to throw off his own. Impatiently, she lifted her arms to draw him back down to her, gasping as he began a trail of kisses that followed an inevitable course along her body.

In the soft light, with the storm carrying itself out to sea, he lifted his head to smile down at her radiant face. "Your eyes are almost black, my love. Shall I tell you why?"

"I have a pretty good idea," she managed shakily, and then she allowed him to sweep away the last remnants of uncertainty on a wave of passion that carried them both far beyond the storm.

Silhouette *Romance*

15-Day Free Trial Offer
6 Silhouette Romances

6 Silhouette Romances, free for 15 days! We'll send you 6 new Silhouette Romances to keep for 15 days, absolutely free! If you decide not to keep them, send them back to us. You pay nothing.

Free Home Delivery. But if you enjoy them as much as we think you will, keep them by paying the invoice enclosed with your free trial shipment. We'll pay all shipping and handling charges. You get the convenience of Home Delivery and we pay the postage and handling charge each month.

Don't miss a copy. The Silhouette Book Club is the way to make sure you'll be able to receive every new romance we publish before they're sold out. There is no minimum number of books to buy and you can cancel at any time.

This offer expires February 28, 1983

Silhouette Book Club, Dept SBS 17B
120 Brighton Road, Clifton, NJ 07012

Please send me 6 Silhouette Romances to keep for 15 days, absolutely free. I understand I am not obligated to join the Silhouette Book Club unless I decide to keep them.

NAME_____

ADDRESS_____

CITY_____STATE_____ZIP_____

IT'S YOUR OWN SPECIAL TIME

Contemporary romances for today's women.
Each month, six very special love stories will be yours
from SILHOUETTE. Look for them wherever books are sold
or order now from the coupon below.

$1.50 each

Hampson	☐ 1	☐ 4	☐ 16	☐ 27	Browning	☐ 12	☐ 38	☐ 53 ☐ 73
	☐ 28	☐ 52	☐ 94			☐ 93		
Stanford	☐ 6	☐ 25	☐ 35	☐ 46	Michaels	☐ 15	☐ 32	☐ 61 ☐ 87
	☐ 58	☐ 88			John	☐ 17	☐ 34	☐ 57 ☐ 85
Hastings	☐ 13	☐ 26			Deckinan	☐ 8	☐ 37	☐ 54 ☐ 96
Vitek	☐ 33	☐ 47	☐ 84		Wisdom	☐ 49	☐ 95	
Wildman	☐ 29	☐ 48			Halston	☐ 62	☐ 83	

☐ 5 Goforth	☐ 22 Stepheno	☐ 50 Scott	☐ 81 Roberts
☐ 7 Lewis	☐ 23 Edwards	☐ 55 Ladame	☐ 82 Dailey
☐ 9 Wilson	☐ 24 Healy	☐ 56 Trent	☐ 86 Adams
☐ 10 Caine	☐ 30 Dixon	☐ 59 Vernon	☐ 89 James
☐ 11 Vernon	☐ 31 Halldorson	☐ 60 Hill	☐ 90 Major
☐ 14 Oliver	☐ 36 McKay	☐ 63 Brent	☐ 92 McKay
☐ 19 Thornton	☐ 39 Sinclair	☐ 71 Ripy	☐ 97 Clay
☐ 20 Fulford	☐ 43 Robb	☐ 76 Hardy	☐ 98 St. George
☐ 21 Richards	☐ 45 Carroll	☐ 78 Oliver	☐ 99 Camp

$1.75 each

Stanford	☐ 100	☐ 112	☐ 131	Hampson	☐ 108	☐ 119	☐ 128	☐ 136
Hardy	☐ 101	☐ 130			☐ 147	☐ 151	☐ 155	☐ 160
Cork	☐ 103	☐ 148		Browning	☐ 113	☐ 142	☐ 164	
Vitek	☐ 104	☐ 139	☐ 157	Michaels	☐ 114	☐ 146		
Dailey	☐ 106	☐ 118	☐ 153	Beckman	☐ 124	☐ 154		
Bright	☐ 107	☐ 125		Roberts	☐ 127	☐ 143	☐ 163	
				Trent	☐ 110	☐ 161		

$1.75 each

☐ 102 Hastings	☐ 120 Carroll	☐ 134 Charles	☐ 150 Major
☐ 105 Eden	☐ 121 Langan	☐ 135 Logan	☐ 152 Halston
☐ 109 Vernon	☐ 122 Scofield	☐ 137 Hunter	☐ 156 Sawyer
☐ 111 South	☐ 123 Sinclair	☐ 138 Wilson	☐ 158 Reynolds
☐ 115 John	☐ 126 St. George	☐ 140 Erskine	☐ 159 Tracy
☐ 116 Lindley	☐ 129 Converse	☐ 144 Goforth	☐ 162 Ashby
☐ 117 Scott	☐ 132 Wisdom	☐ 145 Hope	☐ 165 Young
	☐ 133 Rowe	☐ 149 Saunders	

_ #166 DREAMS FROM THE PAST Wisdom   _ #172 LOGIC OF THE HEART Browning
_ #167 A SILVER NUTMEG Hunter   _ #173 DEVIL'S BARGAIN Camp
_ #168 MOONLIGHT AND MEMORIES Carr   _ #174 FLIGHT TO ROMANCE Sinclair
_ #169 LOVER COME BACK Scott   _ #175 IN NAME ONLY Jarrett
_ #170 A TREASURE OF LOVE Ripy   _ #176 SWEET SURRENDER Vitek
_ #171 LADY MOON Hill   _ #177 THE SECOND TIME Dailey

**LOOK FOR _DARK FANTASY_ BY LAURA HARDY
AVAILABLE IN NOVEMBER AND
MISTLETOE AND HOLLY BY JANET DAILEY
IN DECEMBER.**

SILHOUETTE BOOKS. Department SB/1
1230 Avenue of the Americas
New York, NY 10020

Please send me the books I have checked above. I am enclosing
$_____ (please add 50¢ to cover postage and handling. NYS and
NYC residents please add appropriate sales tax). Send check or
money order—no cash or C.O.D.'s please. Allow six weeks for delivery.

NAME_____

ADDRESS_____

CITY_____STATE/ZIP_____

Silhouette Desire
15-Day Trial Offer
A new romance series that explores contemporary relationships in exciting detail

Six Silhouette Desire romances, free for 15 days! We'll send you six new Silhouette Desire romances to look over for 15 days, absolutely free! If you decide not to keep the books, return them and owe nothing.

Six books a month, free home delivery. If you like Silhouette Desire romances as much as we think you will, keep them and return your payment with the invoice. Then we will send you six new books every month to preview, just as soon as they are published. You pay only for the books you decide to keep, and you never pay postage and handling.

— — — MAIL TODAY — — —

Silhouette Desire, Dept. SDSR 7I
120 Brighton Road, Clifton, NJ 07012

Please send me 6 Silhouette Desire romances to keep for 15 days, absolutely free. I understand I am not obligated to join the Silhouette Desire Book Club unless I decide to keep them.

Name_____

Address_____

City_____

State _____ Zip_____

This offer expires April 30, 1983

Silhouette Romance

Coming next month from
Silhouette Romances

The Tender Years by Anne Hampson

As Christine changed into a woman her feelings toward Luke Curtis changed as well. He was no longer her childhood mentor. Something more was growing between them—something that would alter Christine's life forever.

Mermaid's Touch by Patti Beckman

In her underwater world no problems existed for Amy Peterson. But once she emerged from the Aquarena her problems crashed down around her. Would a no-love merger with Scott Creighton be her only way out?

Island Of Flowers by Nora Roberts

When Laine came to Hawaii to make amends with her father his young business partner tried to thwart the reconciliation. She realized that Dillion must overcome his mistrust of her; for only then would she find his love.

Man Of Velvet by Dana Terrill

Caleb blamed Dianna for Barrett's death and wanted to avenge Barrett through his own loveless marriage to Dianna. Dianna couldn't imagine anything worse—until she found herself falling in love with the man who hated her.

Sweet Eternity by Rita Clay

Brenna had a choice: security, or love with a man who would always be between tournaments—and women. Could she resist his pressure? But then did she really want to?

No Trifling With Love by Mary Lee Stanley

When Connie took a teaching job she hoped her afternoon with the mysterious George Trevelyan would fade from her mind. But her heart told her he was not the type to be easily forgotten.